Adam Andrews Johnson

1

3

The Mantis Variant – Book One
Copyright ©2022 by Adam Andrews Johnson.
Edited by Brent Allan Northup

For information, connect with the author on social media.
Instagram @AdamAndrewsJohnson
Twitter @AuthorQueerotic
Facebook.com/AdamAndrewsJohnson

<u>Acknowledgment</u>

I want to thank Jules L. Grant, award-winning author of dark fantasy, for being so supportive and encouraging. Thank you for believing in my writing, welcoming me on the Book Slam Xtra podcast, and inspiring me to create something on the darker side.

Jason "Fozzie" Nelson, I adore you and your writing! Thank you for being so involved in the art of creating with me.

Adam Andrews Johnson

5

This book is dedicated to Christa,
always waiting for the end of the world.

Agrell regretted her decision. Of course, the ritual she endured was *not* her decision, and a burning resentment now overshadowed the awe-inspired devotion of her childhood. Before the ceremony, Agrell still felt a mysterious sense of wonder. But in the darkness later that night, she muffled the sobs that wracked her body, as she drifted in and out of restless sleep.

In the temple gardens the next day, Agrell smiled and rejoiced with her fellow Messiahs. She hid the confusion and sorrow that was twisting her soul in knots, and Agrell repeated lines that she heard countless other Messiahs say after their own inductions.

"Long live the mantis!" Agrell declared, and everyone replied as they always did.

"Hail, the mantis!" and their words were like smoke in the cold December air.

She had been told since childhood that every Messiah who went through the ceremony became an important member of the order. Each one of them who came before her was now an elder. No one ever left.

Agrell was born and grew up in an isolated community. She was raised to believe that Shifts were an abomination of nature. The forced indoctrination was used to hammer into her brain that Shifts were not even human, and they were inferior to the trueborn. In her earliest years, Agrell believed out of fear what she was told. But that fear soon became curiosity, and what the elders had told her came into conflict with what Agrell began to believe for herself.

As a child, she could not understand why these Shifts were considered evil. Their descriptions made them sound like magical beings. It was unclear to her where they came from, and she was not privy to the arcane wisdom of her Messiah elders. When young Agrell asked questions, she was more often than not met with disdain and dismissal, and she learned to keep her curious nature to herself. Agrell also did not know how Messiahs gained their enhancements, but on her 18th birthday, their secret was revealed.

Agrell's mother led her to the sacred chapel at sundown. No children were permitted within, and this was her first time entering the tiny building. The two were the last to arrive and the room was already crowded.

Those elders who were Agrell's role models and teachers surrounded her, and the leader of the community stepped up and towered over her. He was a large man, with broad shoulders and an intimidating presence. Agrell was used to seeing him from a distance. There were two rooms that helped set him apart and above the other members of the community, one with an elaborate wooden chair and the other with a pulpit from which he delivered his messages.

He looked down at Agrell with a smile, and the ritual began. It came with a shocking revelation.

"The source of Shifts' powers," he proclaimed, "is the mantis gland. This genetic corruption of our pure humankind must be ripped out by the root. It cannot be allowed to remain! The sin of being born a Shift must be cleansed. It is by the removal of a Shift's mantis gland that they are purified, and it is through the consumption of it that we are elevated."

The ceremonial master was dressed in a robe of crimson, and his garment was decorated with brighter red trim at the hems. He wore a sash of burgundy around his waist and a matching scarf draped over his shoulders. Atop his head sat a skullcap that was patterned with vivid roses.

Over one shoulder was slung a long reflective red chain, and beneath the opposite arm was a knife. Its handle was the color of pinot noir so dark that it was almost black, and the weapon was sheathed in red leather set with gemstones that looked like sparkling blood.

He raised his arms, and to Agrell's horror, her young cousin was dragged into the chamber. The boy was just on the cusp of turning 14. He was bound and bruised and bloody. Tears were streaming down his cheeks. He was gagged, and his hands were tied behind his back.

"What?" Agrell began, but her mother grabbed the back of her arm. She gripped it tight and her fingernails dug into her daughter's skin. Agrell held her tongue.

The red priest pointed an accusatory finger at the trembling boy. "This monstrosity," he spat, and his voice took on a wrathful tone, "tried to infiltrate our community! He tried to spoil our sanctuary! You filth," he raged, "show us what evil you can do."

Agrell turned her head and shot her mother a scowl, but the woman did not release her arm. Her mother's gaze was fixed on their leader.

"Do it, slime!" the priest demanded of the child.

The boy choked a sob and furrowed his brow. In the blink of an eye, he disappeared from where he knelt and instantly reappeared by the wall behind the priest.

Agrell was startled.

Her young cousin looked around in confusion. He was still bound. The child turned with desperation in his eyes and stared at the only other person in the room who was not an adult. Their gaze met. Neither he nor Agrell could comprehend what they were experiencing.

"You see?!" Fury flashed across the red priest's face and spittle foamed at the corners of his mouth. Two of his acolytes grabbed the boy. "Once full-grown, this monster would be able to disappear and reappear anywhere! *Anywhere!* Children are not meant to be cursed with powers such as these!" He grabbed a fistful of hair and the boy let out a muffled cry through the gag. The man drew his dagger from its red scabbard, and when he spoke again, his voice shifted and took on a deep monotone.

"It is by the removal of Shifts from society," the man droned, "that we procure the future of the trueborn. It is upon our shoulders that the responsibility rests. The cleansing of this accursed race of subhumans falls to us. We are the eradicators, the purifiers, the sanctified." He brought his knife to the child's throat. "We are not chosen; we are predestined. We will be the ones to wash away the poison of their infestation."

"Please," whispered Agrell in a quavering voice.

Her mother released the grip on her arm, but Agrell was grabbed on both sides by two of the ceremony master's fellow priests. She was forced down to her knees and held there.

"Shifts are a disease against humanity!" the fuming man bellowed. "We take the world one tiny step closer to balance with the removal of each Shift and the uplifting of each new Messiah." He yanked the boy to his feet and shoved him right in front of where Agrell knelt.

She looked up at her young cousin in despair, as the red priest slit the child's throat.

"No!" Agrell screamed, and she was showered in blood. It gushed onto her head, sprayed her in the face, and filled her mouth. The terrible shock of it jolted her into silence, and she spat out the sticky warm liquid.

Her cousin's eyeballs shifted this way and that in their sockets, as his panicked gaze darted around the room from one person to another. His blood covered Agrell. He ground his teeth against the gag in his mouth, and his fluids spurted once more before the boy's jaw slackened. His eyes fell still and became unfocused. Blood bubbled out of his nose and seeped from his restrained mouth.

"We send you where you belong, Shift, to the land of the unliving."

Another elder took the dagger and handed the leader a cleaver.

"Thank you, cousin," the red priest said, and he started hacking away at the dead child's spine. With a snarl on his face, he decapitated the boy. He kicked the limp body to the floor and held the dripping head aloft.

The other Messiah elders erupted in cheers and applause.

"And we make one of our number," the man continued, and the rest fell silent again, "more than she could have been on her own." He handed the cleaver to one of the other leaders. The priest then hooked a finger of his free hand in the gag, and as he pulled it from the mouth, the boy's tongue lolled out.

The ceremony was already appalling to Agrell, but it was about to get worse.

She was left kneeling in a puddle of blood, as a small table was positioned between her and the priest. He placed the boy's head onto the surface, and a fellow elder returned the knife with its red handle to the leader's empty hand.

"Thank you, cousin," the man repeated. He then began peeling the flesh from the bone. "By each removal of an enemy Shift, we move humankind closer to divinity again." Chunk by gruesome chunk, the boy's face and scalp were scraped away, and the skull beneath was revealed. "Our rightful place at the summit has been usurped by these mutilations of nature."

The red priest turned the skull on its side and stuck his knife's tip into the gristly connective tissue at one corner of the jawbone, then the other. He flipped the hideous mess upside down, ripped the jaw from the skull, and then turned it upright again. It sat on its upper teeth.

An acolyte dressed in white took the blade and handed the priest a silver hammer.

"Thank you, cousin," he replied. He raised the shimmering tool above the skull. "To conquer the new enemy of humanity, we need strength!" and the man brought his hammer down.

The grisly head made a wet crunch.

Another assistant stepped up to the table, placed a crystal bowl beside the mangled head, and reverently took the bloody hammer.

The red priest nodded in appreciation. He then stuck his thumbs into both eye sockets and caused the glassy orbs therein to rupture and ooze down the front of the skull. The man pulled both hands in opposite directions, and for a moment, nothing happened. Quiet pops from within the bones indicated that they were about to give, and the skull ruptured. The slick pale pink brain matter sloughed out into the sparkling bowl, and the man discarded the two pieces of the skull onto the floor beside the boy's headless corpse.

Agrell was barely breathing, as the priest thrust his hands into the brains and worked his fingers through the slime.

He continued speaking in his elevated and ritualistically repetitive way. "The aberration of nature that are Shifts, from them comes the source of we Messiahs' power." When he found what he sought in the bowl, his eyes lit up. "For edification, for elevation, for strength and speed, to be more than we once were!" He raised one hand from the bowl and thrust his fist toward the sky. Gore dripped down his wrist.

The table was removed, and the red priest continued. "Consuming the body of Shifts," the man declared, "raises us from our place among the pure and proper humanity, elevating us to Messiahs of the lost, Messiahs of the world."

All the elders said aloud and in unison, "Consume!"

The leader smiled. He lowered his arm and opened his palm in front of Agrell's face.

Among the dripping bits of brain, she could see something different. In the center of the man's hand was a tiny gemstone. He poured water over the crystal and much of the fleshy grey-pink matter fell away.

"Consume!" the elders repeated.

The red priest leaned towards Agrell and whispered a single command.

"Swallow it."

The elders said again, "Consume!" and they all simultaneously stomped one foot. *Thump!* They repeated, "Consume!" and they stomped their other foot. *Thump!* "Consume!" and the group around her continued the slow stomping.

Thump!

Agrell's mind raced. What was this all about?

Thump!

Why did they murder her little cousin and smash his head open?

Thump!

She spent her entire youth anticipating this ceremony, being told that it would be the most glorious day of her life, and the beginning of a new one.

Thump!

Her eyes shifted this way and that over the staring faces of her elders.

Thump!

With a quivering hand, Agrell reached forward and clasped the little gem between her thumb and finger.

Thump!

She pulled the sparkling thing from the gooey bits in the priest's hand.

Thump!

"Consume!" the elders said even louder in their unified voice.

Thump!

Agrell looked around the room again in disbelief, but several of the elders were nodding encouragement to her.

Thump!

The priest extended a fresh glass of water to Agrell.

Thump!

"Consume!"

She stuck the tiny gem into her mouth, caught a mineral-scented whiff of her dead cousin's brains, and she snatched the glass of water from the man. Agrell gulped deeply and swallowed the crystal.

Thump!

The elders stopped stomping their feet.

On her knees and coated in blood, Agrell began to weep.

Then it felt like lightning struck inside her. She cried out in agony and doubled over. Agrell gasped, fell to the floor beside the headless corpse of her cousin, and she curled her body into a tight ball.

Everything burned. Her muscles tensed. Her limbs locked. Her body trembled.

Pain flashed through Agrell's brain and radiated around her being. She pushed herself up to her hands and knees, as another bolt of lightning struck within. She squeezed her eyes shut and screamed. Her skin felt like it was on fire. Agrell felt like she was being melted in acid, and she let out another wail.

All in an instant, the pain vanished. Her screams stopped and her eyes flashed open. She rose back up to a kneeling position and looked around at her fellow elders.

Before she could say a word, one of them drew a broadsword from its sheath and swung the straight blade with terrible fury at the blood-soaked girl. She did not even have the opportunity to get her hands up before it struck the side of her neck.

Agrell squeezed her eyes shut again. In a flash, she knew her life was spent. She did not understand why the elders put her through this ghastly ritual, only to kill her at the end.

She did not feel any pain. Agrell knew she was dead.

A moment passed.

Then she noticed that she was still breathing; she could still feel her own heartbeat. Agrell was even aware of how the blood on her skin was getting tacky as it dried. She opened her eyes.

Everyone in the cramped ceremonial chamber was smiling at her.

She looked down. The blade was partially wrapped around her throat, and there was now a severe warp to the weapon.

The red priest took the hilt from his fellow elder's hand. "Thank you, cousin," he said yet again. He removed the twisted sword from the side of Agrell's neck, allowed one of his knees to drop to the floor in front of her, and he extended the mangled weapon forward.

"You are reborn, Agrell," he said to her. "Now you are one of us. We welcome you as the newest Messiah." He smiled. "You knelt down as a girl, now rise a woman."

Agrell took the broken sword in her hands, without comprehending what she was being shown. She flipped it over, confused by the entire proceeding.

The priest rose and reached out to her.

Agrell took his hand, and the elders burst into more cheering. She stood before them all, wide-eyed and covered in blood.

"It is done," the red priest concluded, and those gathered exited the ceremonial building as the stars above were beginning to sparkle in the darkening sky.

Over the following hours, as that first night progressed, Agrell's confusion boiled up into a rage that then shifted into sorrow. The next morning, she buried her resentment and kept her emotions a secret from those around her.

Throughout that day, as each member congratulated her, Agrell repeated, "Long live the mantis!"

"Hail, the mantis!" they replied with pride.

This was not what the Messiahs had told Agrell for her entire youth. This was not what she wanted. This was not what was right.

Later that evening, a mere 24 hours after she was welcomed into the higher order of her sect and promoted to Messiah, Agrell fled the only home and family she ever knew.

She snuck out into the cold darkness and followed the old road that led to Teshon City. Though she had never visited it before, Agrell was certain that she could escape there and hide among the masses.

She knew that she would forever be haunted by her little cousin's brutal death, and Agrell could not believe how wrong she was in thinking that her home was ever safe ★

Chapter 2 - Dozi, Part One

Teshon City was a slum divided into three boroughs, and each was worse than the others in its own way. Messiahs dwelt in and around the high tower, Demifae mystics were at the waterfront, and the region farthest inland was occupied by Shifts. The industrial district served as workspaces and warehouses for several fringe groups of that society, and many unevolved humans also made up some of the inhabitants in each of the neighborhoods.

The city itself sprang up over two and a half centuries earlier, in an abandoned and derelict military base that was established by the long-defeated and disbanded Oselians. They were a brief but massive empire that fell as quickly as it rose. Their former fortress stood moldering on a small peninsula that extended out into a protected harbor. The natural shape of the land reached out from both sides like a pair of arms that prevented storms and crashing waves from pummeling the spit of rock that housed the base. Warships once found safety in the harbor, but after the fall of Oselia, only tiny fishing vessels dotted the calm waters.

Shacks and lean-tos covered the many docks of the old base, and the haphazard little domiciles looked like they were overlapping each other and threatening to shove their neighbors into the cove. No trees grew anywhere in Teshon City, but spindly grasses and weeds poked up between the cracks of the concrete, especially close to the water's edge. They stretched up for more light beneath the rotting planks of the multiple gangways along the peninsula's coast.

The Demifae inhabitants of the waterfront neighborhood called it the Spritehood. Those mystics and their acolytes, along with anyone else who craved the new magic, dwelt in that region. It also attracted folks who hated Shifts, and there were many excuses that people used for hating Shifts.

*

Dozi lived alone at the edge of the Spritehood. She did not hate Shifts; she just wanted to be more than she was.

Dozi was born in the year 228 A.E. and she lived with the people of the Bluewood Village until her younger brother's 11th birthday. Dozi did not try to convince anyone to come with her when she left; she invited no one, but a local boy insisted on following her. The two were the same age, but he was immature and dimwitted, barely more than a child.

As adolescents they were close, but Dozi outgrew him in their early teenage years. Even into their young adulthood, the boy followed her around the village and the surrounding forests like a pet, and whatever childhood fondness she once felt for him long since faded. When Dozi announced to her people that she was leaving, he joined her. The boy was reluctant but unwilling to let her go by herself, despite her intention to journey alone.

She did not argue with the boy; Dozi never did.

He threw together a makeshift travel sack, while many of their friends tried to convince him not to follow her.

By age 22, Dozi already proved to her fellow villagers how determined she was, and few words were spoken in protest to her departure. In fact, many folks wished her well. She was an important part of that small community, but Dozi's mind and life and future were her own.

With the warm summer sun shining down and birds singing in the treetops, the two young adults set out down a trail they walked many times before. Dozi and the boy spoke very little as they hiked; they had spoken very little over the past few years. He was often in her company, but only as a member of the local rabble who idolized her.

One of the village elders once compared Dozi to the legend of the Pied Piper, with her entourage who were always in tow. Her adoring troops were the saddest ones to see her leave the village. She was like one of those rockstars from olden times, back in those years before the Advanced Era.

Early into her teenage years, Dozi took to dressing in oversized and baggy clothing that she wore layered, even in the summer. She preferred practical and comfortable garments to restrictive or sensual ones. Bulky jackets covered thick hooded cloaks and long-sleeved shirts beneath. Over pairs of shorts, she wore large trousers made of thick material cinched around her waist with a heavy belt. Dozi's hair was cropped short and often covered with a knit hat; she owned quite a collection of them.

Her daily outfits made Dozi nondescript and shapeless, but even as a preteen, there was so much charisma in her personality and swagger in her step that she possessed the confidence to dress the way she wanted. Dozi did not intend to be a role model for the village youth, but she was.

The journey down from the Bluewood Village through the forested lowlands to Teshon City took the people of the hills three days; rugged Dozi was determined to make the trek in two. The boy by her side was a sturdy lad and kept pace with her, and they managed to achieve her goal. On the second night, they made camp with the lights of the city visible in the distance.

The two ate in contemplative silence. Dozi was anxious to arrive at Teshon City, and she was excited to establish herself. Over her teenage years, she made the trip many times into the urbanscape for supplies, and she fell in love with those congested and rundown boroughs at first sight. The city lights always looked most inviting. Dozi would have moved sooner, but she waited until her younger sibling was of hunting age before saying her goodbyes to the people she called family.

However, a rising dread was prickling in the boy's mind. As they were bedding down under the setting sun, he spoke up in a fearful tone.

"Maybe we should go back."

Dozi rolled onto her side, turned her back to him, and replied, "Go to sleep." Neither spoke again.

She may not have been expecting it, but Dozi was not surprised the next morning. In the glow of the sunrise, she awoke to find herself alone. She would not miss the boy.

After a cold breakfast that consisted of a few smoked venison meatballs and a sweet potato cake, Dozi rose and kicked dirt over the coals that still smoldered from the fire they built the night before. She scooped up her two traveling bags and began the last leg of her journey.

An enhancement from the Demifae mystics' studies of arcane arts was something Dozi greatly desired, and their methods required fewer deaths. She convinced herself that the loss of a single Shift life, to enhance a whole host of humans, was worth the sacrifice. For every Messiah, the death of a Shift was required, but the eldritch means that Demifae sorcerers developed to share gifts with unevolved humans necessitated less sacrifice.

Dozi thought of her many childhood visits to Teshon City, where she met people with heightened senses and incredible strength. She saw folks who could communicate with animals, and acrobats who were able to accomplish feats beyond what any normal person could achieve. Dozi even once saw a person with a headful of flames.

With the sun rising over the forest, she passed the minor side trail to Ilin, and Dozi looked toward the ruins of that old castle. She continued forward. Ahead of her, the back of the sign indicating the path came into view. At the end of every trip to Teshon City, Dozi, with the group from her village traveled back home by the Pinewood Path; its sign was always a sad sight to the girl. This was her only trip to the city that did not include a return journey, and as she passed it, Dozi turned back to look at the sign.

It used to be the last part of her visits and meant that she was saying goodbye to the place she loved, but Dozi now felt excited to know she was home. It was not long before she approached the bridge over the Lonely River, and she crossed it with building anticipation. This was what she always wanted, her new home, Teshon City.

Ahead of her, the panels of the old rusted gate rose from the earth like immovable sentinels that greeted all who entered the city. The mechanisms that once opened and closed the entrance were corroded beyond repair, and the doors stood frozen. More than two hundred years before, the gates served as the base's cutoff. Over that time, the neighborhood stretched out around them and the city's limit became vague.

Gate Town, as the locals called it, was a slum but it was also vibrant. It was the most diverse and welcoming part of the city, and Dozi always enjoyed the time she spent there. She intended on living farther in, closer to the water, but she found Gate Town to be fascinating.

Despite the squalor, or maybe because of it, much of Teshon City was decorated. Whole sides of buildings were painted with murals, tapestries and banners blew in the ocean breeze, and people cultivated many species of beautiful flowers. They grew them in the tiny patches of sun, where the beams of light were able to reach down between the old military buildings.

A number of people stood by their dwellings, or behind stalls and served food to the passersby. Dozi wondered which ones were Shifts; most were indistinguishable from their human cousins. Only rarely did a Shift go through a physical change with the onset of their powers, and Dozi's eyes moved from one normal-looking person to another.

Only one of them needs to die, she thought to herself, *and at least the body will be gone before I'm involved*. Dozi did not like to think of it as murder, and she pushed the thought from her mind.

A few inhabitants of the neighborhood waved at her and she nodded, but before long she was through the outer region of the city, and Dozi entered the industrial district. She knew that at night it was best to avoid the area, but she strutted along the old concrete pathways with a smile on her face and the warm morning sun shining down. Between the stone buildings ahead of her, Dozi could see the unique structure that always so intrigued her, the Tower. It loomed ahead.

The chaperones from Dozi's village avoided the Messiahs, but she was not afraid of cannibals; they were not after her. A path ran around the tower's base and she circled it twice, with her eyes turned up towards the imposing structure.

Beneath the decorations that the citizens used to brighten much of their city, the old Oselian concrete was grey. The leadership of the Messiahs left their Tower bare, and the stone structure slowly grew paler under the bleaching rays of the summer sun.

When Dozi was done marveling at the Messiahs' temple, she turned towards the water and left the tower behind her. She knew right where she was headed and entered the Spritehood.

This was where Dozi felt like she belonged. This was where she could forge her new life. This was going to be her home.

The Spritehood was always her favorite part of town, and she now walked by shops and buildings that she passed on other trips. It was exciting to know that now she could pop into any of them anytime she fancied.

She stepped up to the front door of a store that intrigued her on many previous visits. The glass was etched with the words *Abernathy's Apothecary*, and there was a strange symbol beneath the lettering that she was never able to decipher. Dozi was always curious about its meaning. A bell rang as she pulled open the door.

This shop was one of many in the neighborhood that carried the necessities for sorcery, witchcraft, and all magicks. Dozi only ever looked in through the windows, and she thought the assortment of items available was staggering. Abernathy's Apothecary was a tidy and organized space, with tins and baskets full of ingredients. There were vials with liquids in many hues, jars of herbs, and even dried bones tied together in bundles. Several premade potions were also available for sale.

"Umm, Abernathy?" Dozi ventured as the door closed behind her.

"Nope," replied a woman. "What'll it be?"

"Oh, sorry," Dozi responded. "I'm looking for a job and a place to stay."

The clerk pursed her lips. "I don't have either of those," she replied curtly.

Behind the woman, a door burst open and a tall man came through. He was covered in blood. It coated his hands and forearms to the elbows, and there were splatters all over his heavy off-white apron. Streaks of red even made their way up to his facemask, glasses, and surgery cap. Through the door, Dozi saw the source of the blood, and it shocked her.

Sprawled in an unceremonious wheelbarrow was the grey-skinned headless corpse of a man. The hideous neck wound oozed thick dark fluids onto the floor by a metal drain. At the end of its rigid limbs, the body was missing both of its hands and feet. Its genitals were also hacked off, and there were multiple gashes in the torso and thighs. A huge chunk of flesh was missing from one shoulder and the bone was exposed beneath. An overhead light shined down upon the mutilated corpse like it was some sort of exalted monstrosity.

Dozi stood frozen, as the door closed behind the man and hid the body. An iron-like aroma of blood hit her nostrils, and Dozi's nose twitched. She recoiled a little, but her determination overshadowed her other feelings, and she repeated her request to the man.

"I need a job and somewhere to live," she blurted out. "I also want to be a Demifae, but I don't know how."

He flashed her a scowl and snapped in a dismissive tone, "Money!" He then turned to his assistant. "The mantis gland is jarred. I'll take the body. You get started on the mess, and lock the door behind *her*," he added, effectively shoeing Dozi out of his shop.

Back on the street, she adjusted the shoulder straps of her two bags and glared at the sign that the assistant put in the window.

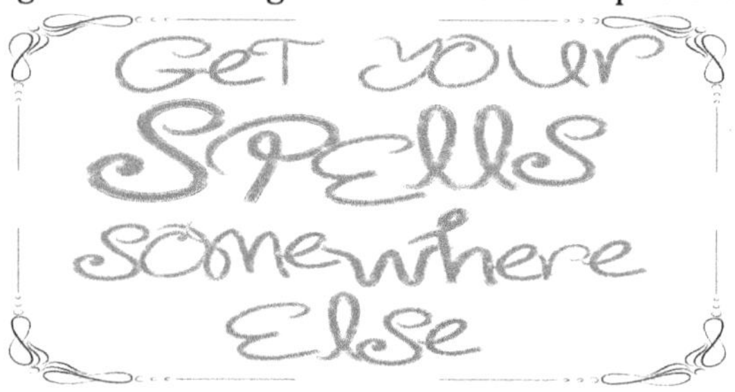

Dozi felt disheartened and headed straight to the water's edge. Having grown up in the mountains, she loved the sea. There were beaches to the south of Teshon City, but the peninsula was a rocky outcropping, ideal for the old military base. The land rose only a short distance above the gentle harbor, and Dozi walked to the trail that led around the edge of the land. She put her hand on the railing, looked down the stone face of the short cliff, and stared into the clear water below. Little fish were swimming close to the rock wall beneath the surface.

Dozi shifted her eyes over to the Oselian Stone Wharf. Several people were fishing from the old breakwater that jutted into the harbor and extended out toward the open ocean. She turned her back to it and began to follow the path along Widdershins Bay.

Across the wide channel, the cliffs rose higher and plummeted deep beneath the surface of the harbor. The waterway had allowed the Oselian navy to dock many of their ships at one time. One of Dozi's childhood neighbors was fascinated by the long-disbanded military. He loved telling old war stories to the children, and the devastation of the Breakneck Shipwreck was one of his favorites. Now as Dozi walked alone, she gazed out at the sunken hulk that protruded from the water a ways ahead of her.

She thought that she ought to make another attempt at procuring a job, lodgings, and magic. However, it was still early and Dozi noticed that most shops were not yet open even though the summer sun was climbing high into the morning sky. She could not decide if it was lucky or unlucky that she found the one open shop with those rude people. Dozi pushed the thought of that horribly mutilated corpse from her mind and continued along until she came to the edge of the Spritehood. The old shipwreck was just a little way farther.

Eventually, she approached the fence that surrounded the wasteland of the Oselian airfield, and she left the main region of the city behind. The tarmac became scorching hot for more than six months of the year, and for the rest of the time, most of the residents tended to avoid it.

Dozi appreciated the solitude and did not mind the heat. She liked the bustle of the city but knew that she would periodically need breaks from it. Alone with her thoughts, Dozi admitted to herself that she did not have much of a plan once she arrived in the city, but she was determined to make her way by sheer will alone.

No railing ran along the edge of the peninsula beside the old runway, and Dozi followed the water until she noticed an area where several boulders were dislodged from the city's foundation. A narrow lip of stone ran along the bottom of the cliff right above the water, and she lowered herself over the edge onto one of the massive stones. Her feet were on a smooth angled portion and they threatened to slip out from under her, but she squatted down and slid onto another lower rock.

Some of the path at the water's edge looked slippery, but Dozi stepped down and followed it. She walked with one hand against the rock wall, which stretched up a little way above her head. After a short distance, Dozi started hearing noise from the city above, but she could not see the people from her position.

She came upon a flat boulder, took a seat, and listened to the indistinct chatter from a distance. In her bag, there was only a single good-sized portion of meatballs and sweet potato cake left, so she chose to eat half of it and saved the rest for later.

Dozi was confident that she would find a place to live; it just might take her some time to meet the right people or locate an unused old military building where she could make a home. She was even willing to sleep on the street for a time if it came to that.

When Dozi finished eating her rationed portion, she continued farther around the water's edge. She did not mind being alone; she was just happy to be in the city. Dozi also did not mind that she did not have a plan. She was confident that she could make her own way.

Bloodwater Falls was ahead of her, and the sun was at its peak in the sky, so she decided to walk all the way to the waterfall before turning back. Dozi arrived at it quicker than she expected and was surprised to see a small chasm in the rock behind the falling water. She attempted to keep her bags dry and stepped behind the waterfall into the protected space.

The noise was deafening, but a moment later she was through to the other side, standing on the stone lip that continued farther around the bay. Dozi knew she should go back, but her excitement about being in Teshon City urged her forward. The path became wider on the far side of Bloodwater Falls, but it was rockier and uneven. Dozi was surefooted from her life in the mountains, and she was an excellent swimmer, so she was unconcerned with the potential of falling into the water, but she did not want her things to get wet.

She continued along the rocks until she began to approach the shipwreck again, but now from the opposite side. Then the sunlight sparkled on something shiny that caught her eye. She bent down, took hold of the glittering object, and gently pulled. A fine silver chain began to emerge from behind a rock, and attached to it was an empty locket. However, the jewelry was only the beginning of her discovery. Behind the stone on which it was hooked, there was an opening in the wall of the cliff.

A dark cave led in and up away from the water. The summer sun was starting to slide toward the horizon, and the slanted light did not make it far into the entrance. However, a crack in the stones overhead sent a bright beam that shined deeper toward the back. It was tall enough within for Dozi to stand upright, and although she saw signs that other people once knew about the cave, it did not appear that anyone was currently living in it. It appeared to have remained vacant for some time.

Exploring as much as she could with the fading light revealed very little, but the cave seemed to extend farther. Then in the darkening gloom, she suddenly found food. Dozi snatched some of it, bit off the tops, and she chewed. The earthy flavors were familiar, almost nutty or meaty. She grabbed another cluster and ate it also. Their texture was a bit tough and they would have been more enjoyable if Dozi cooked them first, but she was glad for something extra to eat.

Over her many trips to Teshon City, Dozi learned that the tide only rose and dropped a few feet in the harbor waters to the north, and the dry stones inside the cave indicated that she was in a safe place, at least for the night. With the hope that no one would stumble upon her while she was asleep, Dozi tried to find a comfortable spot, and she covered herself in a blanket that she took out of her bags. The sunlight soon disappeared, and despite her elation about being in the city and her unfamiliarity with the cave, she was soon asleep.

Several hours later, in oppressive darkness, she woke in pain. Dozi threw off the blanket and gripped her stomach. Her head swam and her mind would not focus. The night was so black that her eyes ached with the strain of trying to see. Her body lurched, and she vomited hard, emptying her guts onto the floor of the cave.

She was dizzy and squeezed her eyes shut, but when she opened them, even the darkness seemed to be spinning. Her isolation forced her into confrontation with the doubts and fears that plagued her mind, feelings that she always kept at bay. They now flooded her with accusations and condescending questions. The negativity manifested like a shadow that twisted her spirit into knots, and the monster took form.

Who do you think you are? it asked her in a voice like a predator. The shape leered at her with eyes of black fire in the dark, and it repeated, *Who do you think you are, leaving everything and everyone you know, leaving the people you love?*

The being of smoke and shadow grew and expanded. It filled the tiny cave, and Dozi's voice escaped her. She could not even scream as the terror enveloped her. The unseen face of fangs and eyeballs and orifices raged at the cowering girl.

Who do you think you are? it questioned yet again. *You are nothing. You are the nothing that's left over. Abandoner. Faithless one. No one wanted you to stay, your family is glad you're gone. Pariah. They're better off without you. You should die in this cave, your body eaten by crabs, your bones to be found by some other worthless pathetic little girl. You will be forever forgotten and lost to time. Deserter. Your name will never be spoken again, nor shall sunlight ever shine upon your face.*

Dozi tumbled into unconsciousness and knew that she would not survive the smothering darkness✪

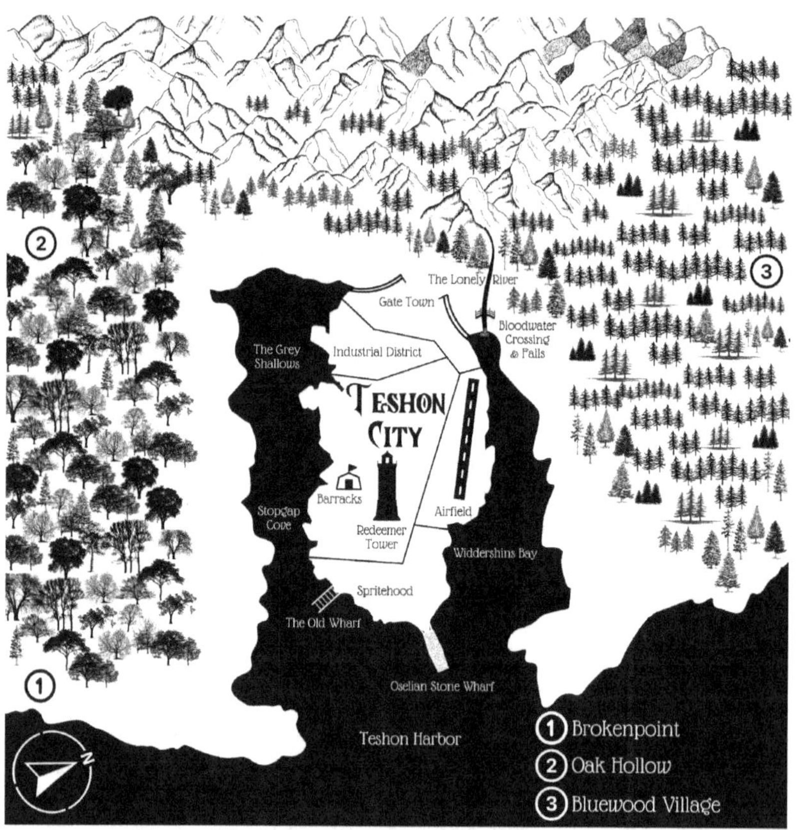

Map of the region surrounding Teshon City

Map of Teshon City & Harbor

Chapter 3 - Ilya, Part One

Very few of the Shift residents of Teshon City dwelt anywhere other than the community they built for themselves, and all were accepted at the entrance of the old dilapidated stronghold. Gate Town, and the neighborhood of Shifton in particular, was a Shift-friendly shantytown that was the poorest region of the city.

Shifts were often abandoned by their families, who did not possess the capacity to love them. The wretched and rejected youth from all around the region would find their way to this welcoming borough. They formed neofamily groups that were more tight-knit than natural families, and sympathetic humans made up a large portion of their community. For almost 250 years, Shifts and their allies hid and protected their own.

No one knew who the first Shift was, but the initial year of their appearance would later come to be renamed Year Zero in the Advanced Era, and the world was never the same again.

Some experts proposed that Shifts were the next step up the evolutionary ladder. Others considered that they were a new, alternate branch of humanity's grand family tree. Those first few individuals, who were recognized as evolved, stood out as unique from the rest of their genetically inferior cousins. For the first time in recorded history, humankind was forced to share the planet with a separate species of hominid.

Shifts are humans born with what biologists dubbed the photonova gland, more commonly referred to as the mantis gland. It is a crystalline-organic structure that resides between the two hemispheres of the brain, in the same location as the pineal in humans. For the first decade of a Shift's life, their photonova gland remains in a state of dormancy as it slowly develops. Soon after the onset of puberty, the internal structure of the gland finishes solidifying, and a tiny trigger mechanism activates. Photonova glands connect Shifts to the energies of the cosmos and provide them with otherworldly abilities.

However, the covetous greed that powerful men felt about those first self-powered individuals led to many hateful and jealous people spreading bigoted ideas. One of the most common and dangerous beliefs was that Shifts were some sort of aberration that needed to be eradicated.

Experimentation was inevitable, and it was soon revealed that Shifts' powers could be stolen. When word got out to the masses, many of the weakest among the early Shifts were tracked down and slain. Groups of hunters sprang up that some people called murderers and cannibals, but they began to refer to themselves as Messiahs.

Humans who consume the photonova gland from a Shift become Messiahs. They are enhanced with heightened speed, strength, and agility. They are made nigh-invincible and the biological upgrade is permanent. In the same way that some saw an inferiority of humans compared to Shifts, these newly enhanced individuals considered themselves above humankind, and their title of Messiah was used to set them apart as well.

Through the rise and fall of the Oselian Empire, and over the following two centuries, the three distinct groups grew more segregated. Confrontation between Shifts, Messiahs, and humans was a constant threat to Teshon City.

*

At the very edge of Gate Town, outside the old base's grand entryway, there stood a sun-scorched shack. A group of several Shifts built it, and they made the tiny building their home in the city's outskirts.

Ilya was 19.

The dry season lasted through the autumn, and the winter rains finally started while she was out collecting supplies. The brief few weeks of wet weather were always a relief to the citizens of Teshon City, but Ilya did not leave that morning dressed for rain, and she returned soaked to the bone. The temperature was dropping, but she was unaffected by the cold.

As Ilya approached the rickety structure with her arms and satchel laden with food and equipment, she scowled at the sight of her home. She and four others built their hovel over two years prior. The shack was hobbled together with driftwood and old rotted planks of decking, and the thing was getting worse for wear by the day. It looked as if it might collapse at any moment; she half-wished it fell while she was gone. Her dilapidated home could barely be considered a hut, yet it housed their group of five Shifts for the time that it stood.

Ilya lifted the tarp that served as her domicile's makeshift door, and she slipped inside. Two young teenage boys were stretched out together on a pile of blankets. Both were infected by the blood corruption. One and then the other developed the virus a mere week earlier. The red sickness was more often than not fatal, and over the course of the previous several days, the boys' conditions only worsened. Ilya steeled herself against the loss of them. She knew it was imminent. Loss was a familiar feeling.

Early into their second year as a group, the eldest member went out to fish in the harbor like he did countless times before, but he never came home. There was also another girl about Ilya's age, and she lived with them for almost two years, until she foolishly fell for a human. She loved him, but his affections were deception. Less than a month into what seemed to be a romantic courtship, her corpse was found headless in an alley.

Ilya's short life was rife with loss. Even her parents abandoned her when it was revealed that their daughter was a Shift. She was only 12 years old at the time.

The cold rain now pattered down on the shanty's roof above her head, and water seeped in at the failing seams. It dripped from the holes in the repurposed boards that were not a problem during the long rainless months.

Ilya set everything that she carried into the driest corner, and she knelt on the floor beside the sick boys. Their wheezing breaths and fitful sleep brought a lump to her throat. One of the last symptoms of the blood corruption was described as madness, but for most ill people, the manifestation was more akin to a failure of their cognition.

During the previous night, the two boys awoke in the darkness, and Ilya was startled from her sleep by the sounds of them talking. Their speech was slowed and slurred, and they mumbled incomplete thoughts and partial sentences, before fading back into fevered unconsciousness. Ilya remained awake after the disturbance, curled up in the dark with her heart breaking.

Now kneeling beside their makeshift bed in the gloomy light from the gray sky that barely illuminated the inside of the shack, she covered her mouth and choked back a sob.

With the rain falling, Ilya's tears flowed.

The boys were both near death. One of them was barely breathing. He started convulsing, and Ilya brought her hands to his shoulders to prevent him from hitting the other boy. He foamed at the mouth and went rigid. His little arms and legs quivered against his sides, and he took a final gasping breath before falling still.

Ilya let out a quiet wail. She took a quavering breath and scooped up the boy's body. She rose and carried him from the hut. He was small and frail before the blood corruption, but now, his corpse was little more than a skeleton in her arms. She walked the few blocks to the edge of the Grey Shallows, and there she left his body to sink into those cursed waters that were poisoned by their history. The boy disappeared beneath the surface.

Ilya turned and headed back into the neighborhood. The winter drizzle hid her tears.

Once inside her hut again, she looked at the final remaining member of her neofamily. The child lay alone, and Ilya could not recall any moment when the two boys were apart. She stared at his sallow skin, his feeble frame, and she gritted her teeth as fresh tears burned from her eyes.

Ilya peeled her sodden shirt up her torso and over her head. She dropped it to the ground with a wet flub. Her trousers were also soaked, and she slid them down her hips and legs, kicking them from her feet. She removed her bra and panties and abandoned the soggy undergarments as well.

For long minutes Ilya stood naked above the dying boy, watching his labored breaths. She was unmoving and steady, but her mind was twisting and trying to arrive at a conclusion.

The food Ilya purchased while she was out earlier that day was not meant for either of the boys. They both had been rapidly progressing along the course of the disease, and neither imbibed food nor drink over the previous two days. Now alone with him, Ilya watched the boy twitching in his sleep, and she allowed her eyes to close.

After a moment, she turned to the corner and unwrapped several pieces of dried meat and two carrots. Ilya ate to the sounds of the rain. When she finished, she again knelt down beside where the boy lay. She placed one gentle palm on his chest and bowed her head. He moaned in his restless sleep and his brow furrowed in pain.

Ilya took a steady breath, reached into her satchel, and her fingers wrapped around the hilt of her dagger. It unsheathed with a hushed ring as the steel slid along the velvety interior of the scabbard. She did not say a word, and with one fell thrust, Ilya jabbed the blade into his left side and yanked it back out again.

The boy's blood did not erupt, it did not spray, but his life flowed out from the wound she inflicted in his heart. The red liquid poured onto the floor where Ilya knelt, and it coated her shins. She stayed beside the boy with her hand on his chest through his brief death throes. His eyes did not open as his life left him.

She sighed and slowly rose and his blood pooled around her feet. Ilya pulled back the flap to the entrance of her home and stepped outside, naked in the rain. She balled her fists above her head, opened her mouth, and screamed her sorrow to the winter sky.

A few people stuck their heads out of neighboring shacks, only to be startled by the sight of her nakedness.

Ilya ignored them. She brought both palms to one of the unsteady exterior walls of her hut, and she gave the thing a hateful shove. The entire tiny structure collapsed with a horrible crash, and she stood above the devastation with the rain gently pelting her skin.

Ilya was a tall woman. She was muscular, an imposing force of nature. Standing bare against the elements and with the sky beginning to darken, Ilya looked like some terrible ancient goddess.

Grief pushed her to be unconcerned in the moment that anyone might see her nudity, and Ilya's crushing sadness overshadowed her fear that someone would realize she was a Shift. Deciding to use her powers for the first time in seven years, Ilya activated her abilities. Her feet lifted off the ground, and she soared up through the clouded skies above Teshon City. She flew high towards the forested mountains and disappeared into that rugged wilderness.

Even while living in the Shifton neighborhood of Gate Town, she kept her powers hidden. Ilya pretended that she was a human, living secretly among her fellow Shifts. She even kept the fact that she was a Shift from her replacement mother.

Ilya was born in the forest town of Oak Hollow, a half-day journey south of Teshon City. As a youth, she was frail and petite, smaller than the other children. She tended to keep to herself. At 12, Ilya was yet to have a growth spurt, and her parents did not even suspect that she was on the cusp of puberty.

It was revealed that Ilya was a Shift when her parents found her asleep early one morning, but not in her bed. Their daughter was curled up and wrapped in a blanket on the ceiling. She awoke to their startled cries, and little Ilya kicked off from the wall as if swimming through the air, and she sailed towards her frightened parents.

The two people, who until the day before loved Ilya with all their hearts, now accused and questioned their child like she was some sort of criminal. They declared that she must have been poisoned by another Shift, and that their daughter could not possibly be one of them. However, as dawn broke, there could be no doubt that Ilya was indeed a Shift, and her parents expelled her from their home.

Ilya's father pushed his daughter out the front door of their hut, and her mother grabbed her by the arm. The two adults berated and ridiculed their sobbing child, as they dragged her to the edge of town. They shoved Ilya onto the path that led out of Oak Hollow, and her father stopped and loomed over her with his arms crossed over his chest. A wicked scowl was scrawled across his face. Her mother gripped Ilya's wrist tightly and continued dragging her farther. She flung her arm and Ilya stumbled and fell to her knees. She wailed as the woman turned her back and returned to her husband's side.

The child's mind barely comprehended the shocking treatment by the people who had loved her every previous minute of her young life.

Through the tears that streamed from her eyes, Ilya could see that neighbors were joining her parents in the cruelty. Their jeering voices mingled and became an indecipherable cacophony of vile words spat at the pitiful child.

Between her broken breaths, little Ilya pleaded not to be sent away.

Her mother picked up a stone, and without hesitation, she threw it at her daughter. The projectile hit the dirt in front of Ilya, bounced, and pelted against her shin. It was neither a strong throw nor a direct hit, but Ilya was injured in her soul. The other adults also began picking up rocks, and with hitherto undreamt fears bubbling up inside of young Ilya, she pushed herself to her feet.

Another rock came sailing through the air but missed the child, and in despair, Ilya began to drag her feet away from the town. She was being exiled from her home, banished by her parents, run off by the ones she loved under the threat of violence.

Ilya could not believe what she was experiencing, as she trudged in the opposite direction of her home. Suddenly a bolt of pain shot through her, and her body was spun halfway around. She screamed and clutched her shoulder.

One of the rocks had hit its target, and the sounds of laughter came ringing out from many folk who were supposed to be her role models.

Ilya stared at them in horror, and she ran.

THE MANTIS VARIANT

More stones started flying all around her. A small rock collided with the back of her thigh, and she stumbled to the dirt. Another pelted her in the ribs. She cried out and urged herself away from the hateful adults, but before she was out of range, a branch came tumbling end over end through the air. She put her arms in the way, and the thing slammed into her. Ilya staggered but continued to run down the path.

She kept looking back and cried out to her parents continuously, but the growing throng of adults menaced her from a distance. Some brandished logs like clubs and threatened to make their way down the path behind the child. The violence was enough that Ilya turned from the town and fled.

It was not long before the voices of her parents and the other adults could no longer be heard, and alone, 12 year old Ilya made her way north. It took most travelers only about a quarter of a day's journey to walk the length of the path that wound through the woods, but it was already past noon when little Ilya's trudging steps brought her to the end of the trail.

She left the forest and stopped to stare at the Great Southtrack and the ocean-side grasses that thrived in the sandier soil and salty air near the coast. Ilya looked east toward the sea, and she could see a blinking light at the edge of the land. She turned her eyes towards the city.

The minor trail from Oak Hollow connected to the Great Southtrack at the edge of the Grey Shallows, and Ilya looked out over those calm waters. Her parents told her stories about the battles that happened there, but in the moment, those memories were far from her mind. Ilya's sorrow kept the feelings of hunger and exhaustion at bay, and she followed the well-trodden thoroughfare toward the urban sprawl. The path ran along the edge of the land and headed straight into Teshon City.

By early evening, Ilya arrived at the outskirts. She was ignored by everyone. At that time in her life, Ilya was very skilled at getting people not to notice her; she was still childish and small. With no money or food or shelter, she wandered the big city, lost and hopeless.

Eventually, Ilya's hunger forced her to start poking through some garbage for scraps of food, and that was when someone finally paid attention to the child.

"No, girl!" came a voice. "Don't you be eatin' that," and a tall skinny woman with grey-streaked hair stepped into the frame of a doorway.

Light was illuminating from her eyes.

"No, child," she repeated in a gentle way. "There's food here, if'n you don't mind some comp'ny."

The light in the woman's eyes faded and went out.

"I could see you through the wall," she said, and added, "my gift," by means of explanation. She pointed at her eyes. "You're most welcome for the evening. We get all sorts here. You can sit back in the kitchen with me," and she ushered Ilya through the doorway.

Beautiful smells hit the hungry girl right in the nose. Her eyes grew wide and she began to salivate. The woman wiped Ilya's hands with a soapy rag and handed the child a fresh towel.

"Have a seat and I'll make you a plate. By the by, I'm Thenorixia, but most folks 'round here just call me Grandma." She did not ask Ilya's name.

Ilya did not offer it.

Grandma gave her a little stool to sit on, and Ilya watched the excitement around her. She was amazed by what she saw.

A man who was helping in the kitchen waved his fingers through a cooking flame, and the fire left the place where it was burning and ignited his hand. He moved it to another pot of food that was ready to be heated, and the flames leapt from his fingertips and began burning merrily beneath the pot.

The man then handed Ilya a clean bright purple carrot with arching greens poking out of one end. He said to her with a smile, "Gnaw on that while Grandma throws summat together for ya."

Several other people kept going in and out of the dining room from the kitchen, and the galley door swung open and closed each time. Ilya caught brief glimpses of whatever was happening in the main part of the restaurant, and she wished she could see it all.

A performer was entertaining the diners by plucking a stringed instrument, and to Ilya's amazement, the notes appeared as forms of light in the air that faded as each sound dissipated. They flashed and sparkled in an array of vibrant colors.

Ilya may have been amazed by what she saw, but after her parents' vicious actions, she was not going to share her powers with anyone. She would keep her abilities a secret; she did not intend on letting anyone know that she could fly.

Grandma left the food she was prepping and headed out into the dining room. Ilya heard her voice but was uncertain about the meaning of the woman's words.

"Don't make me use me powers on you," Grandma threatened with a loud laugh, and other voices joined her amusement.

A few minutes later, Grandma entered the kitchen again. She put together a dish of food and stepped up to Ilya. She could not find the carrot tops.

"Where's the greens?" she asked.

Ilya looked oblivious.

Grandma ventured further. "From the carrot?"

The chef with hands that controlled fire replied to her.

"The wee'n et 'em," he said.

Grandma looked impressed, and she escorted the child through the swinging doors into the main dining room. The space was big, and groups of people were seated at many of the booths and the bar. Grandma guided Ilya to a small table in the corner and placed the food in front of her.

There was a stage at one end of the room, and the musician was on it above the audience. He strummed a few chords and multiple lights blinked around his head and shoulders. Ilya stared in wonder, and Grandma headed back to her kitchen.

One table over, a woman was feeding herself without using a knife or fork; she was not even using her hands. The woman was not looking at her plate of food, but with no explanation that Ilya's young mind could find, she watched one piece of food after another float up from the woman's plate. She opened her mouth, each bite entered, and she chewed it up before the process repeated with the next hovering morsel.

Ilya's stomach growled and she looked down at a brothy bowl of soup. There were fat noodles, chunks of vegetables, and medallions of sausage floating in it. She began to eat, and the rest of that first evening was a blur. Ilya stayed at the table, watching the musician and the diners, until only she and Grandma were left in the restaurant.

At the front door to the restaurant, the chef with fire fingers said something to Grandma that made them both laugh, and she replied to him with a wide smile.

"You're lucky I don't use me powers on you!" she scolded through her chuckles.

He gave the older woman a peck on the cheek and walked out into the night.

She bolted it behind him and then turned back to Ilya.

"You still hungry?" Grandma asked. She brought her hands to her low back, pushed her hips forward, and she rolled her shoulders. She groaned and let out a sigh. "Whatcha think, girlie, you want summat else to eat?"

Ilya still remained silent, but her eyes were wide and she nodded with enthusiasm to be served more.

Grandma chuckled. "All right, why don't you come back into the kitchen with me and we'll see what we can't find ourselves. I could throw together a curry for you or fry a fish. What do you think?"

Ilya's eyes were wide.

"And what should I call you, little one?" Grandma asked. "What's your name?"

Ilya did not reply but her gaze was fixed on the older lady.

"No?" Grandma asked. "I don't blame you," she added with a smile, "can never be too careful." She eyed the child up and down. "What if I just call you *Flower* for tonight? Would that be all right with you?"

Ilya simply stared.

"Would it be all right if I called you Flower?" Grandma asked again.

Ilya nodded.

"Well, now we're getting somewhere!" Grandma said with a laugh. "Let's make some grub."

She poured quite a lot of oil into a pan and fried two fish in it. They were done in a matter of minutes, and she put them on a plate with a little ramekin of dipping sauce.

"Do you mind if I have a bite?" Grandma asked.

Ilya stared into the woman's eyes and shook her head.

"Thanks, Flower," Grandma replied in a singsong voice, and Ilya smiled at being called the nickname.

Grandma snatched one fish and bit its head clean off. She chewed it up with a grin and hummed to herself. This encouraged Ilya to do the same, and she picked up the other crispy snack in her dainty fingers.

"Dip it in the sauce," Grandma encouraged between chews.

Ilya followed her instructions and enjoyed her first bite. It was crunchy and hot and salty and delicious. She ate the rest of both fish.

After placing the plate into the sink, Grandma opened a side door at the back of the kitchen that led to a narrow set of stairs, and they climbed them. At the top was a cozy single room with a faded beat-up old couch and a bed. There was also a small table and two little wooden chairs.

Through the room's only window, Ilya could see the stars flickering in the darkness of the night sky.

Grandma gave her a shirt that was far too large and perfect for sleeping. She helped Ilya change into it, wiped the child's face with a clean damp cloth, and set her up on the couch with a blanket and a pillow. She then made them each a cup of tea, crawled into her own bed, and the two sipped their warm beverages.

"You'll be okay, Flower," Grandma encouraged.

Teshon City was a magnet for the lost, and the woman was well aware of the large population of displaced youth who scraped out a meek survival in the rundown metropolis. Grandma often helped the destitute with leftovers or scraps from her cooking. The sight of children picking through refuse was an all too common one, and she gave to the needy when she could.

"You'll be okay," she repeated, and she hoped that her words would turn out to be true.

The cup of tea looked very large in the frail child's hands. Ilya sipped it until it was gone, and Grandma pointed at a little side table where she could put the empty mug, then she dimmed the lights.

That first night and on many that followed, Ilya thought of her family, but she shed no tears for them. She neither sobbed herself to sleep nor woke up crying in the night. The next morning, Ilya still felt the pain in her body from the stones that hit her, and even more so the pain in her spirit from the rejection by her parents.

Her first few days in the city were a whirlwind of new sights and sounds and experiences for Ilya, but she soon began to find her place. Life was hard, but with Grandma it was good. Early on, Ilya learned to fight. She scrapped with the other orphans and runaways who made up the city's rabble. She learned to defend herself, and on more than a few occasions, Ilya stuck up for those who could not stick up for themselves.

All the while, she kept her ability of flight a secret.

Ilya also went through a major growth spurt that first year and shot up more than a foot. She enjoyed helping Grandma lug huge sacks of sugar or rice or flour back to the restaurant from the industrial district, and Ilya filled out into a muscular young teenager. Her time with Grandma was joyful but cut too short. The two lived together above the restaurant for just over 3 years, until the day Grandma died.

Most mornings, she left Ilya sleeping and attended an early market to pick up ingredients for the meals she served in her restaurant. That day was a particularly beautiful one, with the sun shining and a cool ocean breeze blowing in from the harbor. The market was held on the old wharf and hosted quite a few of Grandma's favorite vendors. She wove through the crowd toward their stalls.

Beneath the shoppers' feet, the old wharf extended out into the harbor above the deepest section of the inlet. Over 200 years before, Oselian ships that sat deep below the waterline were still able to load and unload their cargo without the danger of running aground, but those massive ocean-faring vessels were a thing of the past. The run-down wooden structure was simply too old, and on such a glorious morning, there were too many people at the market.

With the radiant sun shining above, everyone in attendance was suddenly startled by a terrible creak from the wood below. Then the wharf began to bow, and with splintering devastation, a huge section of the market fell into the harbor.

When Grandma did not return that morning, 15 year old Ilya went looking for her at the market. Word of the disaster reached her before she arrived, and she rushed to see what happened.

On that tragic day, 62 corpses were pulled from the water, and among them was Grandma.

Her lifeless expression kept flashing into Ilya's mind as the girl made her mournful way back to the restaurant. It was late in the afternoon when she arrived, and what she found distracted her from the sorrow she felt.

Several of the regulars who would visit Grandma's restaurant multiple times a week showed up earlier that day and found the doors locked. They broke into the place and were helping themselves to whatever they liked.

Young Ilya knew better than to confront them. She was much bigger at 15 than when Grandma first found her picking through the garbage, but Ilya still knew how to not draw attention to herself. She slunk down the alley and kept to the shadows.

The drunkards inside may not have realized yet that there was a set of stairs that led to the upper story, but Ilya knew they would find it eventually. On the outside of the building, she climbed the metal ladder that led to Grandma's window and snuck inside the little apartment.

Ilya grabbed a few things, looked around the replacement home that gave her three wonderful years, and she exited the way she came. She did not look back.

For the following two years, Ilya lived on the streets of Teshon City. She managed to eke out a life for herself, and eventually even made friends. Four of her closest companions turned out to be other Shifts who were also hiding in plain sight and pretending to be regular humans. The five of them formed a fast bond, and their group would come to build that little shack at the edge of the city limits.

A brief two years later, all of them but Ilya were dead ★

Chapter 4 - Agrell, Part Two

Agrell walked in darkness along the path that led away from her sheltered community. The dead face of her little cousin flashed before her mind's eye, and her feet faltered; she stumbled but caught herself. Agrell swore she would never go back.

She trudged through that entire first night of her self-liberation, and before dawn, she reached the edge of the nearest local hamlet. It was so small that it did not even have an official name. The lot of it consisted of no more than an inn, a blacksmith shop, and a market that was only open one day a week. There were also six small houses in a row that lined the edge of a broad field.

All the lights were out, and Agrell hoped the people who worked at the farm and the inn were still asleep. She did not intend to wake them. Those who lived nearest to the community where Agrell grew up were sympathetic to the group's beliefs and lifestyle. There was a chance that if someone caught her there, they might bring her back. Before coming to the first dark house, she crept off the path into the trees.

Agrell was underdressed, and she shivered her entire trek through the night. A white sheet was pinned over a line, and she slipped it off and wrapped herself in it. The white was bright and would draw attention, so she hoped to find something else to cover it. She did not want to stay there any longer than necessary, and when a quick scan revealed nothing else of use, she quietly approached the next house.

Agrell noticed a hatchet on top of an old stump. She snatched it by the handle, hooked it in her belt, and moved on to the third house. A quick scan of the area in the pre-dawn glow revealed little more than an empty back garden.

The inn sat at the end of the row of houses, and as Agrell made her way past the next three properties, she could find no more clothing or anything else of use. She would need to check around the potentially busier building. Agrell was loath to linger or waste any time and hoped to be on her way from the area before anyone was aware of her.

The lights at the front of the inn were lit.

Agrell crept up to the sidewall of the building, made her way along it, and tried to peer in through a few darkened windows. Nothing was visible within and she approached the back of the tavern. There was a glow through a tiny window in a door on the patio, and Agrell could see a row of hooks and a garment. She snuck up in the patches of shadow, pulled the door open with a creak, and snatched the thick material. A hat and a pair of gloves were underneath it, and she took them as well.

The aroma of food being prepared was tempting, but Agrell gently closed the door and darted back into the woods. She pulled the hat onto her head and covered her cold ears, then she slipped her hands into the gloves. They were too big but they were warm. The garment she stole was a hooded cloak with no sleeves, and she threw it over the sheet. A silver buckle clasped at her neck and she pulled the hood over her hatted head. Agrell left the nameless hamlet behind her.

Then realization dawned on her that she was farther away from the community than she had ever been. As the morning sun began to climb up the pale sky, Agrell pulled her stolen cloak tight. The start of winter was only a matter of days away, and the pale glow of the sun above the horizon provided no warmth.

On she walked, and every step felt like freedom, felt like something she was stealing from the community. Whatever blind dedication existed in her youth for the sect of Messiahs who raised her was gone, and she now enjoyed the feeling of taking something from them. She knew she could never go back.

The sun was cresting its zenith when a much larger village came into view. This was Agrell's first time visiting it, but she knew the name before she reached its sign. The elder Messiahs sometimes made the daylong journey from their community, and Agrell was excited about her first visit to the town. She would not be staying here, but she still wanted to see everything that she was warned against throughout her childhood. She passed the sign.

The old village was said to be an evil place full of the wickedness of Shifts, where the most depraved of humanity festered. Eckelton was described by her elders like a boil on the face of the land.

Agrell could not have been more excited to be there.

However, the little village was only a few tired streets and rundown buildings. She walked by several houses and could see people through the windows, but the lanes were empty on that chilly afternoon. There was a large farm stand with one sign that read OPEN DAILY next to another with the words NOW CLOSED.

Agrell was soon at the other end of the disappointing town, and she stopped. She was flanked by a pair of inns that stood across the street from one another. On a table in front of one sat several plates with a little leftover food.

Having eaten nothing over the previous 24 hours, the hunger that gnawed at Agrell focused with pinpoint precision on whatever was there. She snatched up half of a smoked sausage and shoved it in her mouth. She chewed vigorously, swallowed hard, and followed it with a heel of bread and the rind from a chunk of hard cheese.

Mid-chew, a hateful hand grabbed her wrist. Agrell turned with her eyes wide and her mouth full of food, and she stared up into the face of a very large bearded man.

"What have we got here?" he barked with a sneer, and he tried to pull Agrell towards him. Her cloak opened and the man could see her clothes underneath. "You're one of them people from that cult outside of town, ain't you?" the man snapped. He leered at her and tried to jerk her hand away from the empty plates.

Agrell's palms came to the big men's barrel chest, and she pushed.

To both of their surprise, and despite the man being easily three times her size, he flew back and crashed into another table. He sprawled to the ground as dishes clattered around him.

Agrell turned and ran, and the village disappeared behind her. The woods grew thicker as she made her way, and the evening quickly darkened into night. She found no shelter for quite a while, but several hours after sunset, she came to a lonely farm. A light burned in the cottage window, but the barn nearby was dark. Agrell snuck into the aromatic warmth, climbed into the rafters, and fell asleep in the straw.

Sunrise was only a matter of hours away, and she awoke to the sound of the barn doors being opened and a horse making hungry noises. A man with a short gray beard entered the building, gave his horse a couple of pats, and he let the animal outside toward a bail of hay. Agrell could see the farmer scoop some grain from a large bin, and he added it to the horse's breakfast. As it ate, the man set about to a few other tasks, then he led the horse to the field.

Agrell crept down from the loft and began to make her way back to the path that led into the deep forest, but before she reached the trail, a quiet voice spoke.

"Ain't you hungry?"

Agrell spun around, pulled her cloak tight, and made eye contact with a skinny older woman. She was looking out from one of the windows in the farmhouse.

"Don't mind none that you slept in the barn," she said to Agrell in a gentle tone. "Them're some good animals, and it stays warm at night in there. Reckon I've got something I could give you for your journey," she added, "if you don't have no food, and I don't *want* nothing neither," the woman said in a definitive tone. "Just want to make sure you's okay on your way."

Agrell found her voice. "That's very kind," she said. This woman was the first person with whom Agrell spoke outside of her former community.

"We's penniless," the old woman explained, "but we's got plenty to eat." She placed two apples, a small sack of mixed nuts, and three smoked sausages onto a clean hand towel. She brought the four corners together and tied the bundle with a string.

"Save that for when you gets hungry later," the woman recommended, "and have this before you go." She poured a bowlful of thick gruel, tossed a handful of mixed berries on top, and stuck a spoon in it.

The two stood together on the porch, while the warm bowl heated Agrell's hands, and the porridge filled her belly. When she finished eating, she handed the empty dish and spoon back to the woman. Agrell brought her palms together and bowed deeply to her, but she received a confused expression in reply.

"A simple *thank you* is all," the woman responded, and she attempted an awkward curtsy.

"Yes, thank you," Agrell replied. With the makeshift sack full of food for her journey, she headed back to the path that led into the forest.

"Safe travels, girl," the woman called out with a wave.

The sleep and breakfast invigorated Agrell, and she walked along the trail at an energetic pace. It was mid-afternoon when she arrived at a town that she had heard people in her community mention on a number of occasions. However, she could not remember ever hearing of someone visiting the seaside town.

Eckelton was not even listed on most maps, but the long-established village of Brokenpointe was a thriving fishing port that provided a bounty from the sea to the inhabitants of Teshon City.

Busy people bustled between buildings, and most of them ignored the hooded vagabond who wandered through their midst with her head down. Agrell appeared as just another of the countless travelers who stopped briefly Brokenpointe.

"Fresh sea eels!" called out a vendor to the pedestrians around him. "Get your sea eels here! Fresh caught this morning!" His words were like little wisps of smoke in the cold air.

Agrell continued and passed a small library. A few people were seated out front with books and steaming beverages, but through the windows, her eyes beheld more volumes than she could have possibly imagined.

Suddenly music was playing behind her, and she turned to see a little open park of greenery. A group of musicians were seated together in a circle around a fire. Several were strumming stringed instruments and a few others were thumping hand drums. Agrell did not know how long she listened to them. She stood still and wondered to herself how it could be that she was unaware of so many wondrous things in the world.

Her eyes caught a glimmer down at the end of the street, and she turned toward it. Agrell's mind told her what she was seeing, but she could not believe her eyes. She left the musicians behind her, walked one street farther, and came to the ocean. The vastness of the sea's sprawl boggled her mind. Never could she have envisioned such a sight. She stepped out onto a narrow strip of pebbled beach that led to the water and fell to her knees.

Tears filled her eyes, as the red priest flashed into her mind. That man, throughout her whole life, was their community's exalted leader. He led the people in their daily routines. He was the ceremony master and the lord of rituals.

Agrell thought to herself that he was a murderer.

She stared out through her tears at the rolling ocean, and fresh sorrow broke her heart, as she realized her dead cousin would never behold this breathtaking sight. Agrell choked back the lump in her throat, and she spoke to the stony beach and the sea and the sky.

"Why did they keep this from me?" she quavered in a whisper, and her body was wracked by her sobs. "How could they not share all this? How dare they?!" A wave of rage washed over her misery, but it subsided as quickly as it appeared. Agrell gazed out at the sea as her tears freely flowed.

She grew up barely aware of the ocean's existence. There was a river near the community, but that was the only water that she had experienced in her youth. It was entrancing to look out at the expanse of blue before her. Agrell stayed there watching the waves until they started to change color with the setting sun. Every moment of her new freedom was more incredible than the one before.

However, as the light continued to fade, Agrell rose and looked toward the inland mountains and the clouds that hovered above them. It appeared as if some artistic giant reached up and smeared paint across the sky. No sunset she had ever seen decorated the world as much as this one, and it took Agrell's breath away.

Eventually, evening wrapped the land in shadow, and she left the fishing village behind. The path out of Brokenpointe led through the flat coastal lands toward a blinking light in the distant darkness. Despite that Agrell was walking in its direction, it did not appear to be getting any closer or brighter.

To her right, the ocean kept its soothing sounds rolling over the land, and Agrell liked listening to it. Several paces away from the trail on her opposite side, the forest came to an abrupt halt where the soil was too sandy for the trees to grow.

Agrell was grateful to finally be out of the dense woods and have the stars overhead. The landscape close to the path was covered with heather and other low bushes that appeared grey as the moon began to rise. It was not quite full, but it shined bright with no clouds in the sky.

Agrell felt free.

At a fork in the road, standing between the two diverging paths was a waystone. She paused and removed one of the sausages from the makeshift sack that she was given that morning. Agrell stuck the meat in her mouth and bit off the end. It was a little spicy and felt good going down.

Not far ahead in one direction was the blinking light, but the sign on the stone indicated that Teshon City was along the trail that turned east. Agrell decided that getting there was more important than her curiosity about the light.

She ate the rest of the sausage and removed an apple before stowing the remaining food in the hooded cloak and continuing on her way. Under the cold moonlight, the path was clear and the trail led toward the silhouette of mountains in the distance. They looked jagged against the indigo of the night sky.

Agrell did not know how far she already walked, or how much farther she needed to go, but she was free. She had been unaware that her life in the community was a prison, and this new freedom in her was like a heartbeat that she did not know she possessed.

The hour grew later, and the moon continued to slide across the star-speckled sky. Agrell's eyelids were heavy. Her brain felt muddled from the lack of sleep, the limited food, and her recent horrifying experience. She could barely comprehend her past, and she could also not even consider her future. Her mind seemed to have given up, and she no longer thought about or paid attention to her surroundings. The trudge of her footfalls felt endless.

Behind her, a strange sound began to rise in the quiet of the night. Agrell was delirious with fatigue and did not turn around. The noise was a muffled and repetitive thumping that grew only a little louder, but since the sound appeased neither her exhaustion nor her hunger, her bleary brain told her to ignore it.

Then something collided with Agrell and sent her sprawling to the side of the path. The hood she wore blocked her vision, and a solid object smashed against the side of her face. She pushed herself up against a tree trunk and yanked the hood back.

Her eyes flashed wide, as a dark shape grabbed one of her arms. Agrell's head swam and her ears were ringing, and she could see a second shadow bearing down on her.

Unnamed fears froze her to the spot. She did not understand what was happening, or what these shadow entities desired. Then Agrell's terror took form in her mind; it was the red priest and his acolyte. They caught up to her and she was sure they were going to murder her, just like they did to her cousin. She knew the man was going to slit her throat, bleed her out, and decapitate her. Her little cousin flashed into her mind with that expression of utter desperation on his face before death released him from the torture.

Agrell was going to die horribly. She was going to die alone.

The second dark shape reached out for her.

She could not go back. There was a new and desperate necessity, brought on by her emancipation from that isolated existence, and it sparked a self-preservation that flared to life in that moment.

Agrell's free hand came to the hatchet that hung from her belt, and she swung its blade at the oncoming shadow. Chopping wood was a daily part of life in the community, and she knew how to use the tool; she now used it as a weapon. It was impossible to know when the blade was last sharpened, but it sliced clear through the first being with what seemed to be no resistance, and the hatchet's head entered the second shadow.

The hands that held her vanished.

Agrell fell to her knees and burst into uncontrolled sobs that shook her whole body. She was unharmed, and the shadows were nothing, mere figments of her traumatized mind. Long minutes passed, as Agrell wailed her sorrow into her hands. She eventually managed to catch her breath, but new sounds became clear. The ragged noises of gurgling grunts were coming from beside her.

She opened her eyes and beheld the pair of shadows, but also the blood on her hand. The two entities came into focus, and Agrell realized she was wrong about them being nothing. It was not the red priest and his acolyte, and it was also not monsters. Agrell rose to her feet and looked down at a pair of highway bandits who hoped for an easy score.

Her defensive swing with the little hatchet did far more damage than seemed possible. One man's entire middle was ripped open. He gasped at the air and grasped at his spilled intestines that lolled from his abdomen like vile sausages. Shattered ribs protruded from his side, and the pink fleshy balloon of his lung was flat. A hideous laceration in it wheezed out the air he tried to breathe.

The hatchet itself was embedded in the other man. His torso was also cleaved wide open with bones and innards bulging out, and somehow he was missing an arm. It lay at Agrell's feet. His three remaining limbs were seized up and his body twitched and vibrated, as noises issued from between his gnashing teeth, and blood bubbled from his mouth.

Agrell turned from the two ruined men and fled. Adrenaline raged through her body and her legs pumped her away from the violence. She ran hard, but soon the emotion of the experience overwhelmed her, and she again broke down in sobs.

Her body felt electric, but at the same time, she was completely drained. Through her tears, Agrell looked into the trees just off the path. She walked into the woods, and after only a short distance, she collapsed onto a patch of moss between a pair of old trees that provided her a little cover.

In the cold darkness, she cried herself to sleep✪

Chapter 5 - Dozi, Part Two

A series of shrill repetitive noises coaxed Dozi from her delirium. The warm summer sun was shining through the gap in the roof of the cave when her eyelids fluttered open. She blinked a few times, sat up, and adjusted her disheveled clothes. The baggy and layered garments became twisted in her sleep, but she was dry; the cave protected her through the night. She did not know how long she slept.

As Dozi rose and began to explore, she realized that in the hidden space all around her was an assortment of different varieties of mushrooms. One type grew on the walls of the cave. Farther back, there was another species thriving around a little pool of stagnant water with a piece of driftwood that was partially submerged, and even more mushrooms were growing from the old log.

Dozi then noticed the dried-up puddle of her vomit. The mushrooms she so enthusiastically consumed were a psilocybin variety, and they sent her on an internal journey. Her years of foraging in the mountains trained her well, and she should have known better than to just eat a mushroom without determining which variety it was.

Beneath the opening in the stone ceiling, off-white trails streaked down the interior wall, and many psychotropic fungi were growing below them. Dozi then made sense of the harsh noises that were coming from above her head.

The call of seagulls was not one she grew up hearing in the mountains, but every time she was allowed to make the journey to the city during her youth, she felt like they announced her arrival. The gulls always sounded mournful when she left with her group.

Dozi knew that money was a necessity for city life, and that it was not easy to come by, but an idea began to coalesce in her mind.

She reached down and plucked another clump of the very special mushrooms ★

Chapter 6 - Ilya, Part Two

With her bare feet on a thin layer of freshly fallen snow, Ilya stood, swirled by the flurries that blew over the mountains. She knew her ability of flight was somehow connected to the unique gland that she and all Shifts possessed, but she did not understand why her gift also came with a resistance to the cold. Naked in those wintery woods, Ilya was grateful for the added benefit. The snow brushed against her skin and the wind whipped her hair, but she remained unaffected by the chill.

She closed her eyes and pictured the many people that she loved and already lost over her short life. Tears began to burn her eyes, and the droplets were chilled and fell to the frozen ground.

The boy who Ilya stabbed in the heart inside of their shanty was not the first life she took, but then the faces of her parents flashed into her mind and stopped her tears. She was not even sure that the images in her memory were what her parents looked like. Their cruelty was seven years in her past, and in that time without them, she grew into a strong young woman.

Alone on that mountain with nothing, Ilya did not know what she should do next. She did not know where she would go, and she began to walk aimlessly through the pathless tracts of forest. With her bare feet crunching on the frozen ground, her thoughts spun with painful memories, like the snowflakes that swirled around her. Every friend that she had made in her short life was now dead.

Ilya was without food or water, and she tried to convince herself to return to the city. She needed to make a new home, but she did not feel that she was up to the task. Starting her life over, yet again from nothing, felt to her like a repetitive cycle that would never end.

The high mountain forests were home to predators, and in her despair of that moment, Ilya thought she would be grateful for one such beast to appear and end the misery that was her life. She was impervious to the low temperature, but slaughter by the animals of the mountains seemed like a good way to die.

She did not view her abilities and powers as a gift. She did not ask for them. Of course, she did not even ask to be born, forced into life against her will by the two heartless individuals who just happened to be her parents.

Ilya only ever remembered feeling unlucky✪

Chapter 7 - Agrell, Part Three

Oselian society arose in the aftermath of a war that the survivors referred to as World War III. It was different from the previous two worldwide confrontations and in fact was more akin to the American Civil War.

By the year 37 A.E., nations meant nothing, and borders no longer separated countries. Governments collapsed almost overnight, and royal houses that existed for centuries fell to ruin, as families around the world were torn asunder. Siblings rose up against each other, and the lines that divided the enemy factions were never clear or unified. The devastation each side wrought destroyed the world, and that last of the great wars raged across the earth for almost a decade.

In the Oselian histories, they called the conflict the Lost War. They debated the division between Shifts and humans. The conflict was murky, because although very few Shifts fought against their own kind, many humans sided with their evolved cousins.

Around the world, the might of militaries turned their power against what they thought of as a rising threat within their borders. Despite human's expertise at massacring their own kind, they faced firepower hitherto undreamt by any soldier. The vast empire of America splintered, with China and Russia soon to follow. All the most massive of world powers were the first to fall, as they battled their empowered citizenry.

Bullets became obsolete against entire groups of Shifts with electromagnetic manipulators in their midst. Tanks and planes were no more than toys when confronted by masters of gravitation. Entire legions of soldiers were lost into the earth, swallowed by chasms created by tectonic-disrupting Shifts.

THE MANTIS VARIANT

In the beginning, during the first years of the Advanced Era, a small percentage of humans were born with the photonova gland. At the end of the war, after all the wanton devastation, Shifts were no longer an anomalous minority. Their human cousins were on the brink of extinction when the fighting was finally ended.

However, the decimated population of humans grew at an astronomically faster rate than their evolved cousins. Infants born with a photonova gland were always only a single percentage of births in the Advanced Era. Scientists were never able to develop a test that could determine if a prepubescent child was one of the rare Shifts.

After the worldwide confrontation and fall of civilization, the Oselians were the only notable force to rise in power. Small societies began to regroup during the decades that followed the war, and nation-states grew in pockets where the survivors had gathered. One such burgeoning empire was the Oselians.

They began in the ruins of what was once the city of Prague and spread west across Europe without engaging in battles, by convincing their fellow survivors to band together as one. At its height, the Oselian Empire stretched south to Egypt, and north to the Netherlands. They established settlements in what was formerly the United Kingdom and Ireland, but their lands also expanded east all the way to the western edge of India.

In only certain strategic locations did they set up military facilities, and now Teshon City occupied one of their former bases. The Oselian Empire grew fast. It burned like kindling, raging to life and shining bright, but it could not sustain itself. The collected nations of Oselia spread across Europe, but a mere 19 years after their rise, they were already floundering. Oselia soon crumbled to nothing, and their fall was over 200 years in the past; they were all but forgotten.

*

In the cold predawn light, Agrell awoke with a start. A pair of crows was trying to get into the bound towel that held her food. She sat up and flailed at the birds. They squawked in anger and flew away without managing to steal anything. Agrell was relieved.

With the morning creeping over the world, she decided to head on her way and rose from the forest floor. She peeked around the trees that kept her hidden and scanned the road in both directions. No people were visible, and the landscape did not reveal how far she was from the city. Agrell stepped out onto the path and continued.

A thin layer of gray clouds moved in during the night, and the day took on the gloom of the season. Above the forest, mountains rose high, tinted with pink streaks by the light of the rising sun. The land on the other side of the path climbed a steep incline, and for a portion of the journey, it kept the ocean hidden from view. The sound of waves diminished but never disappeared completely. Far ahead of Agrell, the land again fell, and she could see a sandy beach that extended along the coast.

Breakfast that bleak and chilly morning was the second sausage, and Agrell ate as she walked. When she finished it, she munched on some of the mixed nuts. The land beside her that blocked her view of the sea began to reveal what other secrets lay beyond, and Agrell got her first glimpse of the city.

The military complex was transformed over the prior 200 years into a metropolis, and even in the pale light, Teshon City still sparkled like a bizarre jewel. Agrell's eyes were wide with wonder.

She grew up feeling the instilled fears that her elders imposed on her, fears of cities, and fears of the Shifts who dwelt therein. However, no fear from her childhood compared to the terror she witnessed at the hands of the red priest. Not even the tiniest feeling of doubt now prickled in her mind.

As the land opposite the forest continued to fall and Agrell approached the beach, she marveled at the vast tidal flats that stretched between her and Teshon City. She considered that it might be possible to shorten her journey by a significant amount if she were to cut across them. At the edge of the beach, she stopped and stared over the water towards the city.

"Them shallows are treacherous," a man's voice called out from a little way down the path.

Agrell spun towards the approaching individual, and she pulled her cloak tight around her former community's clothes that revealed too much about her. She immediately worried that the man was coming from the two dead bodies, and he was looking for their killer, but then she realized that he was traveling in the opposite direction.

He was walking with a goat. There was a rope around the animal's neck, and it ambled beside the man in an amicable way. The fellow was tall and skinny, with a black mustache and thick shaggy hair that fell about his brow and ears.

"Ain't made for walkin' through," he continued, "and you can count on me with that. The Grey Shallows, folks call 'em. Many a dead soldier made their graves in them low waters. Don't you be walkin' out there."

Agrell stepped back as the man and his goat drew nearer.

"Don't touch me," she ordered him.

"Beggin' your pardon, milady, but I've no interest in touchin' you. I'm just takin' ol' Esmeralda here to Brokenpointe," and he pointed at the goat with his thumb. "Tradin' her for a matching set of engraved solid silver goblets for my husband, sort of a *his* and *his* set."

Agrell did not reply.

"Nope," the man added, "them shallows ain't as invitin' as they may appear. You'll be wanting to stay on the Southtrack all the way to the city." He finished with a, "Safe journey, fellow traveler," and as he and the goat walked past, he gave her a little wave.

Agrell decided that it was probably best to follow the man's suggestion, and she remained on the path. As she walked, she stared out over the tidal flats. The city was bigger and more wondrous than she could have possibly imagined. Little huts and shacks were visible all along the water's edge, and bright murals were painted on many of the buildings. The array of colors was astounding, especially compared to the pious austerity of the community she left.

Agrell's eyes fixed on an enormous tower with smoke rising from the top of it. The structure was by far the tallest building in the entire city, but there were many other imposing structures sprawling across the peninsula. All the while, the massive entry gates of the grand urbanscape loomed in the distance. They stood at the far end of the inlet above the Grey Shallows, where the land rose again to a jagged cliff.

Teshon City was an oxymoron to Agrell, both large and at the same time small. The land upon which the old base sat seemed to be crammed with far too many buildings, but as she approached the high cliffs and the gates, she realized that the peninsula only stretched a short distance out into the harbor.

Even before she reached the entrance, the area outside the city was bustling, and there were more people than Agrell had ever seen. Instead of being intimidated, however, she instantly wanted to be part of the rhythms that pulsated through the streets. She felt like she belonged with the masses. There was even a stink to the city, and Agrell relished it.

She wrapped the cloak and sheet tight and tried to keep her community garments beneath a secret, as she was bumped and jostled by the other pedestrians. She did her best not to attract any unwanted attention.

The path was damp, but it was not raining at the moment, and the clouds did not appear to hold any more rain in them. Agrell was glad that the storm that soaked the city avoided her in the forest while she slept.

The pale sun was low in the sky and barely glowed through the layer of thin grey clouds, but it was already midday when she walked past the threshold of the Teshon City gates. The rusty hinges of the old mechanism looked as if they remained unmoved for countless years.

Her arrival just happened to coincide with the first day of the Frozen Fair.

"Come on, you lot!" a jolly man called. "The Frozen Fair has started. We've already missed the opening performance of the celebration!"

Agrell knew he was not talking to her, but his enthusiasm was infectious. Walking a little ways behind him and his group, she followed them but pretended that she was not.

They passed rows of little dwellings, and Agrell peeked into some of them. There were people in a few of the huts. The group headed through the neighborhood, then they took a street that led to the base of the high tower at the center of the city.

Agrell paused to look up at the imposing edifice of architecture, but as she did, she heard music.

Every winter solstice, Teshon City held a three-day festival on the Oselian airfield that the people called the Frozen Fair. Even during the coldest part of the year, temperatures in the city seldom dropped below freezing. Nonetheless, folks bundled themselves in their warmest clothes, and they came from each district to the base's single airstrip for the celebration at the beginning of winter.

THE MANTIS VARIANT

What remained of the old tarmac was cracked and broken with patches of dead weeds between the chunks of blacktop. The asphalt became scorching hot during the summer, so most of the city's inhabitants avoided that part of the peninsula during the rest of the year.

Agrell followed the music and other noises of jubilation, and it led her to an enormous crowd. She was not used to so many people but was excited by all the new sights and sounds and smells, and she realized she was smiling.

Whoever was in charge of the decorations went all out for the celebration. A huge section of the former runway was sheared clean of its weeds, and tall poles with torches at their tops lined the area. Banners waved above many stalls in the winter breeze that blew in off the harbor. Some folks offered snacks, while others sold trinkets and handmade wares of all sorts.

Agrell's eyes were filled with wonder. In the isolated camp where she grew up, the group's uniformity dictated that they all wear the same matching clothes. Everyone wore their hair long and the men kept their faces shaved. The sameness in everyone she knew growing up, compared to the vast array of diverse humanity that was thriving in the city, shocked her. Agrell did not know why her family and those who she once considered friends wanted to keep all this *life* away from her.

Then she heard something she was not expecting.

"250 years of Shifts!" someone declared.

Agrell did not know what the person said before it, and their voice was gone again beneath the murmur of the countless throngs who were enjoying the winter market. Agrell was also uncertain what their words meant, and she tried to suppress the sayings from her community leaders that bubbled up in her mind.

Shifts are an abomination. They are a sin against nature, the memories whispered to her. Agrell shook her head.

"If you think this is fancy," a man said right beside her, "wait until you see what they've got planned for the neighborhood!"

He was not talking to Agrell, but she focused on him.

"There's going to be a huge party in Shifton, and folks are going to show off!" he added.

Agrell turned, and to her amazed confusion, she saw a pair of shiny silver balls orbiting the man's head. They circled in opposite directions with a smooth and steady movement.

"I'll be there," a second man confirmed. He stuck a large joint into his mouth, raised one hand without a lighter, and extended a finger toward the end of it. The man's fingertip illuminated, and he sucked. The joint ignited, he pulled smoke into his lungs, and the glow from his finger disappeared.

Agrell was uncertain what she heard and saw, but she stayed focused on the conversation.

The man with the joint took another pull and handed it to his companion. He exhaled a cloud of smoke up into the air above their heads.

"Two and a half centuries," the man marveled, "feels like we've been around forever. Has it really been only 250 years?"

We've been around? Agrell thought. *They're 250 years old?*

Another cloud ascended as the other man exhaled. He coughed, then replied, "Yeah, that's all, 250 years. I can't even imagine what the world was like before us."

Before us? Agrell stared at the two men.

They ignored her.

Then someone called out, "Hey, skinny girl! Yeah, I'm talking to you!"★

Chapter 8 - Dozi & Agrell

Before the evolution of Shifts in the world, magic was relegated to the realms of fantasy and myth, but that all changed in the Advanced Era. In those first few decades before the Lost War, scientists made some startling revelations. They realized early on that not only did consuming a Shift's photonova gland provide the eater with invulnerability, but those researchers who experimented on the glands also were able to perform what many viewed as miracles.

Over the decades, those who tested the limits of what was possible by using the glands, adopted for themselves old and abandoned monikers. They called themselves alchemists and mystics, and an entire subculture arose around them.

THE MANTIS VARIANT

The connection to cosmic energies in photonova glands allowed those who manipulated them to perform wondrous feats that indeed seemed to many like magic. These neo-alchemists provided a plethora of lesser charms that allowed them to achieve things, which people who used to call themselves witches wished they could have performed.

Potions for love or endurance or wisdom were common concoctions. Among those enchantments often requested of mystics were spells that gave a person an advantage over their enemies, or helped couples to conceive, or assisted one in finding lost items.

It required only a single photonova gland for mystics to produce a vast quantity of potions and spells. However, the alchemists eventually learned how to use a fresh gland to perform enhancements on unevolved humans. A single gland allowed a few dozen humans any number of incredible abilities, but the powers stolen were always far inferior to the abilities of the Shift whose life was taken. Enhanced humans saw themselves as above their homosapien brethren, and they took for themselves a new name. They called themselves Demifae.

*

"Hey, skinny girl!" Dozi called over the noise of the Frozen Fair crowd. "Yeah, I'm talking to you!"

Agrell's attention turned from the two men that seemed to be discussing being 250 years old, and she focused on a young woman vendor behind a table of mushrooms.

"You look like a fish out of water," Dozi stated, "and you're one serious string bean, kid."

Agrell thought that she looked no less of a kid herself.

"You're right out in the middle of things. Come back here with me and get out of the way. I'm Dozi," she commented, as Agrell followed her instructions.

She stepped up next to Dozi and pulled her cloak tight. Agrell was not ready to have anyone else recognize where she was from by her community attire.

Dozi was in baggy and bulky clothes. There was a knit hat on her head that was blue and white with sparkling thread woven through it. She wore a confident smile and looked right into Agrell's eyes.

"You lost, kid?" Dozi asked her. "Looks like you've never been to a market before." She chuckled.

"I never have," Agrell replied. "This is my first time."

"Well, then welcome! It can be a lot," Dozi commented, and she looked around at the busy fair. She grinned. "There are so many people here, and this is the first day of the festival, so everyone is excited about it. It's one of the highlights of the year. I've been selling mushrooms at markets around the city for a few months now, but this is my first Frozen Fair as a vendor."

Dozi was not providing much opportunity to reply, but Agrell was feeling rather dumbstruck. The overstimulation of the Fair was intense and she was grateful to be behind the table with the other woman. Watching the festivities would allow her to get her bearings.

"If it's your first time," Dozi asked, "are you new to the city?"

Agrell did not answer and stared out at the people and other vendors. Performers in bright costumes danced and played musical instruments while they sang songs.

"I'll take that as a *yes*," Dozi replied to Agrell's silence. Then a customer approached to purchase mushrooms.

Agrell watched the exchange take place, but she was far too distracted by the exciting festival to pay close attention to what was happening with mushrooms and money. The customer was older, a tall man with broad shoulders and a thick beard with a little gray in it. In the community of Agrell's childhood, no one ever grew out their facial hair. The customer was wrapped in a heavy jacket with a fluffy collar; his hands were gloved and a thick hat was on his head. He smiled at Dozi, as he handed her several coins, and Agrell thought that the man's eyes were very bright. He tucked his purchase into a sack and bowed to Dozi, and then he also bowed to Agrell. She did not know how to respond, but then he turned and mingled back into the crowd.

A dark-skinned woman all in white meandered down the row of vendors. Her body was curvaceous, and she swayed as she walked. She looked radiant in her wintery ensemble. Not only were her coat and leggings white, but her boots and gloves were white as well. Even the hair that crowned her head was as bright as the snow that sometimes fell on the highlands outside of Agrell's former community. The woman peeked at the wares offered by one seller and then another, and she smiled at Agrell and Dozi, as she passed the table of mushrooms.

Suddenly a fireball flashed off to one side, and Agrell was amazed to look over and see a man breathing flames. He was not accomplishing the feat by spitting a spray of oil from his mouth in the direction of a torch, but instead, the man was simply blowing a jet of flames into the air like a dragon. Nothing else about the man appeared reptilian; he did not have a tail or horns. He just seemed to have the natural talent of expelling fire from his mouth. Agrell was in awe.

She then got a taste of the city's darker side.

"Boy!" roared a man in a voice that Agrell could tell was full of rage. "Knock that Shift shit off and keep it in your own fucking neighborhood!"

Dozi said under her breath, "Oh, great, Messiahs."

Several scowling individuals shoved their way through the happy crowd. They were bearing down on the firebreather.

"We have no interest in seeing whatever disgusting shit you can do," continued the man. He bulged with muscles and stood a head above his companions. "Keep your damn mouth shut. If you spit fire again, you'll deal with us."

Before the growling man could say another word, a jet of flames roared right at the gang. However, instead of delightful little fireballs, now it was like a blast furnace. Chaos erupted, and all around, people began screaming and fled for their lives.

The flames hit the oncoming beast of a man in the chest. He put his hands up in the way, but he roared as the blaze ripped into his empowered Messiah flesh. Even being a Messiah was not sufficient protection against the onslaught. He fell to his knees, as his arms disintegrated to scorched bones before Agrell's eyes. The blast raged into the huge man's chest and peeled his body open like the petals of a hideous flower. He was eviscerated by fire, until his head bobbed and rocked and then flopped back, barely still connected to his neck.

The flames vanished and the firebreather shut his mouth.

Sprawling on the ground like some sort of otherworldly extra-dimensional being of twisted flesh, the meat of the Messiah man's upper body was roasted away by the blaze. Smoke curled from the charred bones that protruded from it.

Agrell's eyes were fixed on the deadly encounter, and she did not see the other approaching enemy, as one of the smoldering corpse's companions snuck up to the firebreather from behind.

Then everything went horrible.

A woman kicked him in the back of one knee and it buckled. He stumbled to the ground, and flames again came scorching out of his mouth, but she uppercutted him in the jaw. His mouth slammed shut and smoke came out of his nose. He coughed, then turned his flames toward the woman, but she was armed with a dagger and stabbed him in one eye. His blaze shot wild, spraying around the fair, and several people were hit by the inferno. More screams rang out across the old airstrip.

The scuffle grew worse, as the woman stabbed the Shift in his other eye. He clutched at his face, maybe wailing in agony, but the roar of the flames that gushed from his mouth muffled any sounds he made. His fire burned down the festival.

Agrell was agape and staring, appalled by what she witnessed. She stood frozen, and her mind flashed back to the murder of her cousin, mere days ago.

Fingers gripped into her arm.

"Let's get the fuck out of here!" Dozi shrieked, as she stuffed her mushrooms back into their carrying case.

"What is happening?" Agrell yelled over the commotion.

"Later!" snapped Dozi. She slammed the lid of her case shut, grabbed Agrell's hand, and dragged her away from the chaos.

Agrell looked back and saw the Messiah woman with her knife. She was standing over the firebreather and wearing a hateful smile. He was dead. Like the red priest, the woman now sliced deep into the man's neck. Flames continued to sputter out of his mouth, even though his life was spent. One terrible yank severed the firebreather's head from his shoulders, and the fire died as well. She gripped a fistful of hair in one hand and raised her knife in the other. The woman then licked the blood from the blade.

Dozi tugged Agrell away from the violence and down an alley. The two women made their way along a narrow path with buildings looming above them, and as they wove through the city, more than one panhandler reached out and begged for whatever they could spare.

They rounded one of the base's old warehouses, and the two young women stopped in their tracks as they were confronted by a lecherous old drunk. He was leaning against a wall, mumbling incoherent syllables, and slobbering on himself. His trousers were unzipped and one hand was down his pants. When his bleary eyes focused on Dozi and Agrell, he started making animal noises and pulled his sweaty hand from his waistband. He clawed for them, as they tried to slip past, and he caught hold of Agrell's cloak.

She pulled to free herself, but inadvertently caused him to stumble against her, and he slung an arm over her shoulder. The man leaned into Agrell, sloshed some of his booze onto the pavement, and he pressed his dirty face to hers. His stubble prickled her skin. Then he licked her cheek.

Agrell caught a whiff of the sharp spiky aroma of alcohol, mingled with putrescence from whenever he last vomited. His tongue felt pasty against her face. She recoiled in disgust and her hands found his torso. Agrell pushed him with all her might.

"Let go of..." Dozi started, but her voice vanished.

The man flew back, his body smashing into the wall behind him. The bricks cracked and the mortar between them buckled from the impact. His eyes glazed, blood seeped out of his ears, and he wheezed his final exhale as he slid down the wall.

"What the fuck?" Dozi mumbled in shock. She scanned Agrell, and noticed the hidden clothes beneath her cloak. She grabbed Agrell's hand and raced off around another corner, repeating, "What the fuck? What the fuck?" She turned down a few more alleyways, then finally stopped running and held up her hand. Dozi shook her head and said to herself, "I must be out of my damn mind." Then she added to Agrell, "Come on!"

Dozi led her quite a ways through the neighborhood until they ducked under the overhang of a building and stepped into a shadowed corner. She turned to Agrell with her fists on her hips and arms akimbo.

"You're a Messiah, from that cult?" she asked. Without waiting for Agrell to reply, she added in a shocked voice, "You really did it? You actually went through it?"

"Went through what?" Agrell replied.

"You're one of them, right? You're a Messiah?"

Agrell dropped her head but did not answer. Her little cousin's dead face was tattooed behind her eyelids, and she saw him every time she shut them.

"I mean," Dozi continued, "isn't there only one way to become a Messiah?" She hesitated, and despite that no one else was around, she continued at a whisper. "You ate a person?" Even in the gloom, Dozi's expression looked shocked and incredulous.

Agrell exploded with pitiful sobs and she fell to her knees on the dusty floor of the alley. Her face dropped into her hands, and her long hair draped down around her fingers. She wailed into her palms with her arms trembling.

Dozi was caught off-guard by the outpouring of emotion. Agrell's body shook with her sorrows, but Dozi put a gentle hand on her shoulder. Agrell immediately leaned into the other young woman. She wrapped her arms around her waist and cried against Dozi's stomach.

The layers of thick clothing that Dozi always wore provided a soft padding against which Agrell sobbed her sorrows, and although Dozi felt awkward, she put her palms on Agrell's back. She looked down at the skinny young woman and tried to soothe her, uncertain of what caused the reaction.

After Agrell released that tiny fraction of her overwhelming pain, she was again calm, and Dozi spoke to her in a quiet voice.

"Whatever you went through was not your fault," she comforted. The immense shame that Agrell felt was palpable to Dozi, and she was not going to blame Agrell for anything the cult did.

"It was my decision," Agrell whimpered.

Dozi grabbed both sides of the cape that Agrell stole and tugged it open.

"Hey!" she cried out in protest.

Dozi ignored her. "But you're from that cult, aren't you? I know your people's clothes."

Agrell did not understand the word Dozi had now used twice. "We are Messiahs," she replied and pulled the cloak tight again. "I was born there. I was..." she hesitated, "I was raised to believe that Shifts were an abomination of nature. I was told that I would take part in our blessed ritual," her voice broke, "but they murdered my cousin! He was just a boy and they killed him!" she wailed. Fresh tears burned her eyes. "They murdered him," she said again, but then her voice dropped to a whisper, "and I was covered in his blood. They cut off his head right in front of me."

Agrell kept speaking through her tears. "The elders surrounded me, and they were chanting when they broke open his head and took out his mantis gland. All of them were staring at me and they kept repeating the word and stomping their feet, and I did it!" she blurted out. "I did it; I swallowed it!"

Agrell balled her hands into fists and screamed. It echoed through the empty alley, and Dozi's gaze shot all around the streets, worried about who might be drawn to her cries. Then Agrell fell silent again and took another ragged breath before she spoke.

"I made the decision," she declared. "No one forced it down my throat. No one made me swallow it." She growled through gritted teeth, "Why did I do it?"

Dozi repeated herself in a gentle voice. "It wasn't your fault," she reiterated. "That horrible thing was not your fault. What the cult put you through..." and her voice trailed off, as she tried to ease Agrell's suffering, but Dozi could not help feeling a twinge of jealousy.

That mantis gland could have empowered a lot of us humans, she thought to herself, but guilt instantly washed over her for even thinking it. She cradled the distraught young woman who lost her cousin, and although Dozi felt a little awkward doing it, she gently stroked her fingers through Agrell's hair as she sobbed✪

Chapter 9 - Ilya, Part Three

Night fell on Teshon City. It spread over the mountains that thrust up toward the sky, and the stars began to sparkle to life.

Ilya walked naked through the snowy forest in the darkness. She did not sleep. Throughout the night, her many dead friends entered her mind, and she was more than once brought to tears. There were several people from the days when she lived on the streets, whose faces she could still picture, but their names were lost to her memory.

Above the frozen treetops, the grey sky began to lighten with the slow approach of the early-winter dawn. Snow was still falling, and the sun was hidden behind thick clouds. A layer of fine white flakes covered everything, and it gave the woods an ethereal quality.

Hunger eventually began to nag at Ilya's stomach, and she again activated her powers. Her bare feet lifted from the icy forest floor, and she rose naked into the atmosphere above the jagged mountains and sprawling lands below. She turned towards the distant coast with the vast sea beyond, and Ilya flew.

Her flight would take a fraction of the time it would have required to walk, and although it was years since she last used her powers, they now made her feel something new. It was not that there was a new ability within her, but as the cold wind whipped around her bare form, for the first time, she reveled in her gifts. Why she did not do this sooner, fly up into nature to get away from the city and people, Ilya did not know.

The exhilaration that coursed through her body and radiated down her limbs was incomparable to any feeling she had ever experienced on the ground. Using her long-repressed powers was like making love to a deity. Even true love did not feel like flying, and she once experienced deep love with another, but that painful memory was something for another time.

Right now, Ilya flew, and nothing could diminish the joy she felt embracing her abilities. She ran her fingers over her bare skin, above the trees, as the cold breeze caressed her. Even the bleakness of the pale sky held beauty for her, while she soared through it, and Ilya could not remember a single moment in her life when she felt more elation.

Then the wicked edge of a hunting arrow glanced off her face. The arrowhead ricocheted against her cheekbone, whizzed away, and fell into the trees below.

Ilya screamed in pain and clutched at the bloody gash in her flesh. She focused her powers to stay aloft, as her gaze darted around the forest below.

"Don't hit the head you idiot!" someone yelled down in the trees off to one side.

Ilya launched forward with her untested powers and urged them to their limit. She soared toward the water with the trees whipping below her.

Another near-miss made her veer to one side in midflight. The second arrow sailed high above her and arced far into the distance.

Her eyes focused on the glimmer of Teshon City and she flew hard. With no practice, her powers barely felt like they were in her control, but she knew she needed to go faster.

Then, like being struck by lightning, an arrow found its mark. Ilya gasped in pain that was so fierce it stole her breath. She began to plummet from the sky.

The voices came from behind now, but she did not want to meet the ones who spoke.

"That got her!"

Ilya begged her powers to take her farther, but the trees were coming up fast from below.

"She's dropping, boys!"

A vicious steel shaft with feathers at its end protruded from Ilya's side below her ribs.

"That naked bitch is ours!"

She gritted her teeth and forced her power to obey her command.

"We'll take her head and sell her mantis gland for a pretty piece of copper!"

Ilya pushed her ability and stayed aloft. The forest swept away just beneath her dangling feet.

The coast drew nearer, and the distance between Ilya and the hunters was growing at a pace that they could not match. When the tree line broke and a sandy beach stretched out in front of her, she came in for a landing. Whether due to pain or exhaustion, her powers sputtered at the end of her flight, and Ilya crashed to the soft sand.

She cried out in agony but knew she could not remain there and pushed herself to her feet. With one hand clutching her face and the other on her side, she began to hobble in the direction of Teshon City. She could see in the distance, where the sand became rocks and the land rose away from the water. That stony shore would lead her back to the city and medical attention, and she needed a professional to deal with her horrible wounds.

Ilya was leaking a trail of blood that she knew would be easy to follow, once the hunters made it to the coast. She could not dither, and when she arrived at a path that led inland to the main entrance of the city, Ilya opted to follow the rocks that ran along the water's edge instead. She hoped the stone path would bring her straight to the Spritehood and the mystics that dwelt there for healing.

Beneath the primary lighthouse of Teshon Harbor, Ilya came to a small section where the rocks were underwater. She tried to activate her powers again, and although she could feel them within her, they would not respond. Tentatively, she stepped into the water. One of her feet slid on the slippery rock, and Ilya wailed in pain, as her body wrenched and twisted. She grabbed the arrow, gritted her teeth, and managed to get her feet under her. Slowly she made her way to the drier rocks under the Noreaster Light.

The pain in her side radiated through her entire body and caused stars to flash at the edges of her vision. Her head swam, but step by agonizing step, Ilya forced herself forward. She made her way on the rocks along the northern edge of Widdershins Bay, until she passed the old shipwreck.

Eventually, the waterfall at the end of the deepwater cove by the city gates came into view, and she released a sob of relief. She also felt an overwhelming wave of exhaustion, and with buckling knees, she staggered against the cliff wall beside her. Ilya groaned at the arrow in her side. She hobbled along, keeping one hand on the rocks for support, but then she stumbled upon a small dry cave.

Her spinning brain decided she should rest for a moment in its sanctuary, but as she arrived at the mouth, two young women stepped out and surprised her.

They were also very startled.

"Oh, my gosh, you're naked!" one of them squeaked.

"You've got an arrow in you!" the other one declared with wide eyes.

Ilya fell to her knees at the sandy entrance and reached out to them. She tried to ask for help, but her voice vanished, and she was swallowed in darkness ★

Chapter 10 - Agrell, Dozi, & Ilya

"You've got yourself quite a little savior," Dozi commented, as Ilya opened her eyes.

She tried to sit up.

"Whoa, take it easy, girl," Dozi encouraged.

Ilya's eyes were unfocused, but the pain in her side was a precision fury, like being electrocuted. "They're coming," she groaned.

"Oh-ho," Dozi chuckled in disbelief. She gave Ilya a confused look and replied. "Don't you worry about them. Agrell's done them right. I told her they were after you for your mantis gland, being a Shift and all, and well, you won't need to worry about that lot again." A thought came to Dozi and she added, "Mind you, when we leave this place, don't look back the way you came. Straight towards the city is key. I'm Dozi."

Ilya slowly began to gain her bearings. The wound in her side was making it hard to think, though it seemed to be under control. She looked around.

Dozi was kneeling beside her.

Ilya was still naked but she was wrapped in a large hooded cloak. The arrow was gone and the wound was dressed with some torn cloth as a makeshift bandage.

"How did you know that I..." she began, but Dozi answered her before she could finish.

"The men who did that to you eventually tracked your blood trail to the rockway along the water's edge. You were unconscious." Dozi pointed at the shaft and feathers of the arrow; its head was missing. "A little while after we dealt with *that* shit, we could hear men arguing. We headed out of the cave and they started shouting at us that there was a dangerous Shift who came this way."

Dozi made another perplexed face, shook her head, and continued. "Well, turns out our girl Agrell has a gentle side for people in unfortunate situations, and a very tough side for people who hurt Shifts."

"You've lost some serious blood," Dozi added, "but the wound actually does not seem to have done much damage. One of the mystics in the Spritehood will know what you need, but for now, you've gotta regain your strength a little before we head back out. Do you think you could eat some of this?" and Dozi held out a cold meat pie. "It's not much, but it'll fill you up. I made it myself."

Dozi continued, as Ilya took a bite, "Now, look, whatever you think, Agrell's not who she appears to be. She's new, and she's lost, and nothing that's happened to her is her fault. You've got to understand that and look past the thing that you're likely to realize first. She's *not* what you think."

"I don't understand," Ilya said thickly with a mouth full of food.

Dozi gave her a worried look. "Just don't believe what you're eyes tell you," she reiterated.

The meat pie was gone after another few bites, and Ilya said, "I think I can stand. Thank you for that."

"Let me help you. Take it easy. We found some driftwood that might work as a cane or crutch to help you walk." Dozi rose and assisted Ilya in slowly getting to her feet.

The injured young woman gasped in pain and gripped firmly into Dozi's arm.

"It's okay," Dozi encouraged. "I've gotcha. What do we call you?"

"Ilya," she replied through gritted teeth. Tears trickled from her eyes.

They positioned the wood under her arm, and the two stepped out into the sunshine. The grey of the day before was now only a smudge on the horizon.

"It's morning?" Ilya asked.

"Yeah, you slept through the night," Dozi confirmed, as Ilya inadvertently looked back up the rockway towards the beach.

Agrell was standing with her back to them and looking out at the ocean. A pile of mangled flesh sat on the stones behind her. The sun shimmered off a massive red smear on the wall, and miscellaneous body parts were strewn around the rocks at her feet.

Ilya recognized Agrell's garb at once. "*She's a Messiah from the Lovegood cult?!*" she squawked, but the exertion sent a fresh bolt of pain raging through her body and she leaned hard on the crutch.

"No," Dozi corrected gently, "she was born and raised at the Lovegood cult, and forced into becoming a Messiah when she turned 18, which was just a few days ago. They cut off her cousin's head when it turned out that the boy was a Shift, and after they made her become a Messiah, she ran away. She's been in the city for less than 24 hours."

Dozi added, "I think she was picturing the leadership of the cult while she was pulling those men's limbs off. She squashed one of their heads against the stone wall like it was a grape." Dozi sucked air through her teeth and shook her head.

Ilya just stared.

"You should have heard the screaming," Dozi commented in a voice that almost sounded wistful. "*Hers* I mean. They were screaming too, of course, but her fury was quite something to hear." Dozi added in a guilty tone. She sounded bemused. "I watched it all; I watched as she slaughtered them. She'd been such a quiet girl," but then Dozi turned to Ilya, "and I told you not to look," she said with a scolding tone. "Let's get you out of here. *Agrell!*" Dozi called out, "We're leaving!"

Standing with the sun beaming down on her, Agrell looked like a statue, a seaside sentinel, staring out to greet the ships returning to port. She turned and approached the other young women, and Ilya realized that Agrell was just a skinny little thing who stood a full head shorter than her.

"Are you okay?" Agrell asked in a timid voice. She looked up into Ilya's eyes. "I took that arrow out of you."

"Thank... you..." Ilya said with an unsure voice, eyeing Agrell's blood-soaked body.

Dozi nodded to her in encouragement.

Ilya asked, "How did you remove it?"

Agrell's face lit up. "I held the shaft where it was sticking out of your back, crushed the head in my bare hand, and I snapped it off. Then I pinched in the bit where the metal was sharp and twisted, and Dozi carefully pulled it out. She bandaged you up."

"But it's only temporary," Dozi added. "Enough talking for now. Let's get you back to the city."

"Would you like me to carry you?" Agrell offered.

Ilya looked down at the scrawny and bloody girl with an expression of disbelief and disgust.

"I'm really strong," Agrell added with a little uncertainty in her voice.

"Wait," Dozi said to her, "turn your clothes inside out. That will make them, and you, less recognizable to anyone in the city."

Agrell looked appalled.

"She's right," seconded Ilya. "You stand out in your cult garb."

"If you don't want to be noticed," Dozi added, "the first rule is, don't stand out. Go on," she urged.

The two women stood and stared at Agrell, waiting for her to switch her clothes around so they could be on their way, but she did not move.

"I can't," she whispered, "take my clothes off."

"We don't want you to *take your clothes off*," Dozi said with a skewed look. "We want you to flip your clothes inside out so you blend in more."

"But I can't just get naked!"

Ilya opened the cape that they gave her and revealed her bare body beneath it, bandages and all. "No one is asking you to get naked," she said without closing the garment. "Suit yourself, but I knew who you were immediately. I mean not you personally, but I know you from your group, and others will as well." She winced at a fresh shock of pain in her side and clutched the makeshift crutch.

"I can carry you," Agrell mumbled, while she pulled her top up over her head. She was wearing a bra, but she still tried to cover her small breasts as she turned the shirt inside out. She yanked it forcefully back over her head, slid her trousers off her narrow hips and again tried to prevent herself from being seen before pulling them back onto her legs.

"Better," Ilya groaned to her through gritted teeth.

"Yeah," Dozi agreed, "the blue that everyone in your group wears is recognizable." She caught herself. "Sorry, your *former* group," she corrected. "Also, now the orange thing on the front is hidden. Inside out, the colors are subdued and the symbol is not eye-catching, like it was."

Agrell tried to push aside her discomfort at having been exposed, and she re-stated her offer to Ilya. "Do you want me to carry you back to the city?"

The two of them may have appeared odd, with skinny little Agrell carrying much larger Ilya. However, she weighed almost nothing in Agrell's slender but empowered arms.

"Did those men take your clothes?" Agrell asked in a nervous voice. "Did they do something to you?"

"You mean besides shoot me?" Ilya mumbled. She moaned against another electric flash of pain in her side, gasped, and squeezed her arms tight around Agrell's neck. "No," she said between struggling breaths, "they didn't take my clothes."

THE MANTIS VARIANT

It was not long before the three young women arrived back at the edge of the Spritehood. Carrying Ilya was less convenient once they were on the narrow streets between the old military buildings, and she again walked with the crutch. It was not long before they located a mystic healer and entered the shop.

Behind the main counter, a round man was seated in a large leather armchair. As he stood, it turned out that he was not much taller than Agrell, but easily more than twice her size. His hand shot up above his head and he wiggled his fingers at them in greeting. He was chewing a large mouthful of fluffy white cake with thick creamy frosting, and as he smiled at them, his cheeks bulged out like a chipmunk. The jolly fellow covered his mouth with his hand and rolled his eyes in an apologetic way. He then moved around his counter and swallowed.

"I'm sorry, dear ladies. I confess that you caught me right in the middle of a bite. Now, how may I be of service to you?" He was already peering at the oozing bandage on Ilya's face, but she opened the cape again, exposing her nudity and also revealing the much more serious wound.

The man immediately jumped into action. "Take her in the back, now," he commanded Agrell and Dozi, and he pointed to a door behind him. Then he started naming off things to himself that none of the women recognized. "Chiapple blood, calcium of the vigortree, Durga seeds and bark shavings. Let me see, let me see, there it is. Put her on the examination table," he called to them, "but get rid of that filthy cloak."

Agrell took the cape and looked away from the naked woman.

Ilya cringed as she sat on the cushioned table and leaned back. She stretched out and made no effort to cover herself.

Agrell kept her eyes averted.

As the man entered, he grabbed a fresh sheet and whipped it open. He spread it over Ilya's torso so that only the wound on her side was exposed.

Agrell appreciated his courtesy.

"What happened to her?" he asked, as he daintily removed the bandage Dozi had made.

Ilya winced in pain and sucked air through her teeth.

Dozi nudged Agrell's foot and spoke aloud to the man before she could answer. "We don't know what happened to her. We found her outside the city limits and helped her get back."

"Nasty bit of work, this," the mystic commented, peering down at the wound. He looked up into Ilya's eyes. "You're lucky, doesn't look like it hit anything important," but then he added in a sympathetic tone, "except you. Now, I'm sorry to make you do this, but I need you to sit up," and he put a hand behind her shoulders in assistance.

Tears streamed down Ilya's cheeks from fresh agony that radiated in her side, as the man helped her rise to a seated position.

"Drink this. It's a shot of whisper vinegar. You won't like the taste, but it'll do the trick for now."

"I'd go for a bite of that cake," Ilya mumbled in reply, but she obeyed. She gulped down the bitter beverage and swallowed, sputtering and coughing.

"You can have a whole slice of cake when we're done, my dear," he replied in a soothing voice.

He helped her rest back again as her eyelids began to flutter.

Dozi and Agrell watched their new companion as she received the mystic's ministrations. He made a thick paste from several ingredients and dipped two pieces of gauze into it. Very gently, he packed the wounds at the entry and exit point under Ilya's ribs. He then spread some sort of thick sticky substance like tree sap over both openings and covered her side with fresh clean linen bandages.

The mystic removed the sheet, and Agrell looked away as Ilya's naked body was again exposed. He put a wrap around her ribs that went under her back, and he fastened it in place to hold the bandages secure, then he immediately covered her again with the sheet.

The little round man turned to the other two ladies. "She can rest here," he said, and he waved Dozi and Agrell toward the front of his shop.

A lone individual was perusing the available wares and gave the three of them a little wave when they emerged from the back.

"Let me know if you need anything," the mystic called out to his customer, who nodded without looking back.

He then addressed Dozi and Agrell. "Would either of you like a piece?" and he waved at his half-eaten cake.

Dozi responded right away. "Oh, yes, please, we'd each love one."

The mystic smiled. He scrubbed the blood and ointment from his hands in a basin of water, then he withdrew a box from beneath the counter. He opened it to reveal most of a cake. There was only a small amount missing.

Dozi returned a wide toothy smile to the mystic and extended her hands toward him with her palms face-up.

The fellow removed slices of cake and set them onto two faded and chipped pieces of porcelain flatware. He placed one plate into Dozi's hands, put the other on the counter in front of Agrell, and handed each of them a tarnished little silver dessert fork.

"My husband's birthday was yesterday," the man said with a beaming smile, "but he's not big on sweeties like I am," and he rubbed his round belly before he shoveled another large bite of cake into his mouth.

Dozi dug right into her slice, but Agrell was unfamiliar with anything like the fluffy cloud of pale crumbliness, nor its shimmering white frosting. The cakes she grew up eating during the very few high celebrations each year were things made of dense dough with too many dried fruits. They were drizzled daily in a high alcohol-content plum brandy for three entire months, and the end result was barely palatable, even though everyone in the community said how much they enjoyed the cakes. They commented on how lovely they looked, and how impressive it was that this or that member put so much time and care into the cake, but Agrell always thought they were terrible.

She now pressed the edge of the old silver fork into the frosting, and it sliced through the spongy dessert like it was little more than air. Then she put the bite in her mouth, and it was indeed *much* more than air. This cake was unlike anything Agrell had ever eaten. Its sweetness was delicate and its texture was silky. She thought it was like eating honeyed cream that was whipped into a fluffy mass of perfection.

Agrell's eyes lit up with an emotion that was foreign to her. The delicious decadence made her feel like she was floating, made her feel like she might drift right out the door and sail off into the sunset. Her brain felt sparkly, and she said thickly through her first bite of the treat, "Wow, thishh ishh really good." She swallowed. "This is cake? The only cakes I've ever eaten were nothing like this."

Dozi nudged her below the counter where the mystic could not see, and she said, "You're right. I've never eaten cake this good either!" Dozi knew that she would need to have a talk with Agrell about the way she reacted to all her new experiences.

"I think I'll just help myself to another little wedge," the mystic said as he finished his piece, "so that you two aren't eating alone." He smiled wide and added another slice of cake to his plate.

*

Clear across Teshon City, a pack of hunters that called themselves Talin's Talons were closing in on their prey. The scouts tracked the man for more than a week, a Shift that they claimed possessed the ability to harness devastating cosmic rays from his eyes.

Static crackled before one of them informed the others, "It's veered off course! Repeat, it has veered off course. The docks at the industrial district are no longer its destination. Your current positions are obsolete. It is now headed for Springwater Square."

"Move, hunters!" Talin ordered. He reminded his crew, "The Shift will look exactly like a human. There will be no distinguishing features that set it apart from you or me," he paused, "that is, until it's blasted a pair of holes in your torso. Claw One, you have the lead."

More static hissed.

"You all know that we need to take the Shift out immediately," Claw One instructed. "Do not give it the opportunity to activate its ability or we will lose soldiers. Claws Six and Seven, you're with me to the west. We'll come in from the top and position on three of the buildings around Springwater Square. Two, Three, and Four will approach separately on ground level from the east. Claw Five and Talin will be our backup. Let's move! Get to your new positions!"

Moments later, three of them were climbing ladders to the tops of buildings, while the other three each laid eyes on their target. The square was quiet with the night slowly darkening.

The hiss of static was followed by multiple voices.

"Do you see it? Confirm."

73

"I see it."

"It's entering the square."

"We can't see it yet from our position."

"Hold."

There was a pause.

"Engage," Talin ordered.

His hunt pack was made up solely of Demifae. They moved in, and Claw Three reached their target first. He grabbed the man by his shoulder, spun him around, and hit him in the face. With the steel gauntlets that Claw Three wore, it was like being punched by a brick. His attack dealt a devastating blow to the man's cheek, crushing the bones in his face and knocking him back. He fell to the pavement unconscious.

However, the defensive blasts that were fired from the man's eyes as a reflex also hit their target. The cosmic energies only appeared as a flash to Claw Three's fellow hunters, and then they saw their fellow hunter standing motionless with his arm extended in the punch. Behind him, the pair of plasma projections punched deep divots into the thick wall of one of the old concrete buildings before the energy from them dissipated.

Claw Two stepped up to Claw Three.

His body trembled for a moment, and then it fell to the dusty street.

"Pity," Claw Two tutted down at him.

The few civilians in the square ran from it in terror.

Claw Three's neck and his shoulder were pierced with a pair of smoldering holes about the width of a large coin. The cosmic rays had cut clear through his flesh.

Claw One began to descend from the top of his building, and Claws Six and Seven followed. They joined the other hunters in the square and ran toward Claw Two.

She stepped up to their bloody quarry, put the heel of her boot on his neck, and pressed her toe to his cheek. She held his head against the pavement to keep his eyes pointed away from her. Her face was suddenly full of horrible rage, and she drew a blade from her belt and thrust it into his heart.

The man's eyes flashed open and multiple blasts fired against another one of the buildings. Concrete particles were sent flying around the square like shrapnel, but Claw Two ripped the blade out of his chest, and blood gushed from the hole. His energies failed him, as he gurgled and coughed up his life's fluid, and he was dead.

"Shift filth!" Claw Two spat, and she took her foot from his throat.

Talin and the others ran up to the murdered man and their dead companion. "Dammit," he growled. "Leave the body of Claw Three here and take that Shift's head."✪

Chapter 11 - Home

Ilya awoke in shocking pain and unfamiliar surroundings. She moaned aloud and shoved herself to a seated position. The sheet that covered her fell away from her upper body. She was on a padded table in a small cluttered room. Shelves were lined with countless jars and boxes of herbs and shells and dead insects and seedpods. Dried fish hung from the ceiling in one corner and a large clock adorned the wall directly in front of her.

Ilya's head was spinning. She did not remember where she was, but she looked down and saw that her wounds were bandaged professionally, although the hole through her side was agonizing.

"Hello?" she called out weakly.

A man's muffled voice replied, "I hear you, my dear!"

The door to the room opened and the little round mystic entered.

"Cake guy," Ilya managed.

"Yes, indeed," he said in a gentle tone, "and I've saved a piece for you, but how are you feeling?"

"Like I died," she groaned.

"Luckily, today was not the day for that. Your friends here have waited for your recovery."

"Friends?"

"Remember us?" Dozi asked, as she entered behind the man. "Glad you made it."

"Tophilogin says you can stay here for the night," Agrell commented, as she came through the door, "so he can keep watch over you and give you fresh bandages in the morning." She saw that Ilya was uncovered and looked down.

"Yes, my dear," the man concurred, "if you are alright with it, you really ought to rest and you may stay here. And I already told you," he added, turning to Agrell, "you don't need to call me that."

She furrowed her brow. "But it's on your nameplate out there," and she pointed back toward the main part of his shop.

Dozi interrupted. "That's okay, mystic, we've got a place for her."

"We do?" asked Agrell, and Dozi elbowed her in the ribs.

The mystic turned to Ilya. "If you decide not to stay with me, please come back in the morning and I will re-dress your wound with fresh gauze and ointment, and allow me to loan you a shirt and pair of trousers." The man went through another door and collected some of his clothing from a closet.

Agrell turned her eyes away from Ilya, as she exchanged the sheet for the outfit. She set the garments beside her.

"Sorry about the blood," Ilya groaned, and she swung her legs over the side of the padded table. She gripped the edge of it as a wave of pain and dizziness washed over her.

"Easy!" the mystic said, and he brought a hand to her shoulder for support. "You've lost a lot of blood."

"I'm okay," Ilya managed.

"You most certainly are not," he replied. "Let's get you dressed and get some cake in you. *Then* we'll discuss your okayness."

Dozi and the mystic helped Ilya gingerly slide the shirt over her arms and head. It was far too wide and a bit short, but she wore it with the collar draped off one shoulder, and she did not mind showing off her midriff.

"These shorts will just have to do," the mystic said in an apologetic tone. "They are going to be much too big. Here's a belt to help." He slid the shorts over her feet and up her legs to her thighs.

Dozi let Ilya lean on her to help the injured woman stand.

Ilya pulled the shorts up the rest of the way, cinched them with the belt, and she groaned at her wounds. Then her hand came to her cheek in an inadvertent and self-comforting gesture, and she rediscovered her other injury.

"*Argh!*" she squawked. "What the fuck?!"

"Be careful!" the mystic said with deep concern in his voice. "You have a more minor, but still serious wound on your face."

Ilya let out a moan. "I didn't even feel it over the pain in my side." She grimaced, then she asked in a low voice, "Do you have a mirror?"

The mystic scurried to the front part of his shop, grabbed a small decorative mirror that hung on the wall behind the counter, and returned. He handed it to Ilya. "Your face is bandaged as well," he warned.

Ilya looked at herself and repeated in a murmur to no one in particular, "What the fuck?" She added, "I almost lost my eye!"

The wound started in the middle of her cheek and traveled up to the edge of her orbital socket. It was covered by a thin strip of bandage.

"What the fuck?" she whispered one more time to herself, as she handed the mirror back to the mystic. "Thank you," she added in a dejected tone without looking up at him.

"Now," he said in a calm voice, "how 'bout that cake?"

They helped Ilya hobble out from the back room, and when she was a few bites into the treat, the mystic commented, "Lucky these two found you."

Ilya looked at Dozi and Agrell.

"They didn't seem to know how you came to be in such a horrible state."

Ilya scrunched up her face in concentration, flinched, and caressed the bandage on her cheek. "I'm trying to remember, myself."

"I think she needs to get some rest," Dozi interjected. "We'll take her home and be back tomorrow morning like you said. She'll have her own clothes again and we can return yours to you."

"That's very kind," the mystic said with a nod, "and you'll be able to take care of her?"

Dozi ignored his question and asked, "You're a Demifae, right?"

"Why, yes, my dear. I received my enhancement back in year 214," he said proudly. "I suspect that's before you youngsters were even born."

"You got that right!" Dozi confirmed. "How old are you?" she asked the little round man.

He flashed her a coy smile. "Don't you know that it's impolite to ask a dame her age?" he teased.

When Ilya finished her cake, the mystic provided her with a proper crutch, and he sent the ladies on their way with a sleeping potion to help Ilya get through the night.

Dozi slowly led the two women through the streets of the Spritehood, with Agrell helping Ilya along. Dozi whispered to herself, "I'm out of my mind." Then she turned back to the other two. "Look," she said to Agrell and Ilya, "I'm going to welcome you into my place, but this is all I own, you understand? I live here, and everything I have in the world is here." She stared at them both for a few silent seconds, then she turned.

In a narrow space behind an old ventilation fan cage, there was a small hidden door set below the street line. One woman after another slipped into the gap behind the fan, and they each ducked through the entryway. A set of stairs led them down to a dark basement where a single candle was burning. Dozi lit several more and the room took on an acceptable level of gloom.

She looked at Ilya and then at Agrell. "You two are both *more* than I am. You're a Shift, and you're a Messiah. I know, I know, against your will," Dozi added in a supportive tone. "Just please don't take advantage of me. I'm only a human, and I'm just trying to help."

Dozi pointed toward her cot and assisted Ilya down onto it. "I know it's not much," she said, "but you'll sleep better on my bed than the floor. I'll prep your potion."

Then she focused on Agrell, and Dozi grabbed the skinny woman's arm. "You," she said, "we need to talk." She shoved Agrell towards the area that served as her kitchen.

"I get it," Dozi whispered to her, "you're going to experience a lot of new things in the city, but you cannot draw attention to yourself. Every time you're surprised by something, your reaction will call you out."

She continued. "And as much as the mystic has helped, I don't fucking trust him. He's used Shift mantis glands over the years," Dozi stated, and she turned towards Ilya. "In the same way that you need to keep yourself a secret, she's a Shift, and he can't find out that she is. Do you understand?"

Agrell nodded. Her eyes were wide.

"We will need to square away the story of how she was injured, so it doesn't bring attention to the fact that she's a Shift."

Dozi's head swirled with mixed emotions. She thrust them to the back of her mind.

"Listen, Agrell," she continued, "I really think you should focus on observing, and try to keep most of your thoughts to yourself; they are going to reveal your secrets. I know there will be things that seem interesting, but keep those thoughts to yourself in order to keep your past hidden."

The two of them returned to the main part of Dozi's home. She put her hands on her hips and stood before them both.

"There's plenty of room down here," she said with a little uncertainty in her voice, "and you're welcome to stay with me as long as you need." She turned to Ilya. "Here, let's find you something that fits for tomorrow. I have a dark shirt that won't show if your wounds bleed a little, and it'll cover the bandages on your side." Dozi placed a pair of shorts on the cot beside Ilya, then she helped her remove the mystic's clothes, and Agrell turned away.

Ilya gasped with the effort, and fresh tears sprang to her eyes. "Potion," she managed through clenched teeth.

"They're in my bag, skinny girl," Dozi said to Agrell. "The mystic gave us two vials that need to be mixed before she takes it. He said to just pour one into the other, and that it doesn't matter which way you mix them. Then shake them up."

Agrell lifted the satchel's flap and the two vials were sitting at the top. They were wrapped together in a cloth and each was sealed with a cork. She tried not to pay attention to the other items in the bag but noticed a wad of cash in a metal clip, a knife, and several tins with handwritten labels. Each of the vials was less than half full of liquid; one was clear red like watered-down wine, and the other held a thicker golden substance with the appearance of honey. Agrell pulled the corks from each, poured the red fluid into the other, then resealed it. She gave the potion a shake.

"Here you go," Agrell said, as she removed the cork again and handed the potion to Ilya, who sucked the concoction down.

"Tastes like oleander," she mumbled.

"What does that even taste like?" Dozi asked.

Ilya replied, "I don't know," and her eyelids fluttered as the potion started to work.

"Let's get you tucked in," Dozi said to her, and she pulled up the blanket. Then she turned to Agrell.

"Come on, skinny girl. Let's let her sleep. Got some food over here, if you're still hungry after that cake."

Agrell followed, and mumbled to herself in a tone of disbelief, "This is my first time in the city."

"You've experienced quite a lot over the past day, haven't you?" Dozi replied.

The two of them sat together at a small table and Dozi poured them each a glass of dark ale from a large jug.

"You want a meat pie?" she asked, and without awaiting a reply, she unwrapped two of them. "I think it's goat," Dozi said, and she slid one in front of Agrell.

"Thank you," she replied and took a bite.

Dozi nodded with her own mouth full of food.

They ate in silence, and when they finished, Dozi grabbed a few more articles of clothing. "We need to get you out of that cult garb," she stated, and again, she used the word that was unknown to Agrell. "Here's a shirt and proper trousers." Dozi did not turn around.

Agrell stood there holding the clothes, but she did not move.

"Look, skinny girl, I don't know what it was like in the cult where you grew up, but you don't need to worry about me." She added, "It's *men* you've gotta watch out for."

Dozi peeled off her own three bulky shirts and thrust her pants and shorts below her knees. She stood upright, wearing just a burgundy bra and black panties that did not match.

Agrell was surprised to see how curvaceous Dozi's body was; her breasts were large and her hips were round and sensuous below her narrow waist. She was womanly, and Agrell felt boyish beside her.

Dozi kicked her trousers from her feet. She then folded and hung up her clothes, and swapped them for a pair of soft sleep pants and a large shirt.

"We can use your cloak as a blanket," Dozi encouraged, and she took the garment from Agrell's shoulders. "We'll spread the sheet you've got onto some extra blankets for a makeshift bed," she added.

Agrell very much wanted to get out of her community's clothing, but she was hesitant to disrobe. Though she was concerned with being naked in front of another person, Dozi did not once look over at her as she changed.

On the floor, at the foot of her cot, Dozi set up a thick pile of several blankets. She waved at them and whispered, "We're all women here, skinny girl. We've got to look out for each other."

Agrell stretched out and Dozi spread the cloak over her. She then snuggled down onto the pile of blankets next to Agrell.

An emotion that was so commonly tapped into during Agrell's childhood came flooding back to her. She felt guilty, but guilty for the comfort she was feeling beside this other woman. Dozi opened her home to two complete strangers, and Agrell was feeling things that were foreign to her.

She might have used the word *friendship* or *optimism*, but those were not ideals of the community. The feelings made her feel uncomfortable, and she liked them. Agrell felt safe with Dozi beside her, as she drifted off into dreamless sleep.

A mere matter of hours later, while it was still dark, the three women were awakened by the terrible reverberations of an explosion ★

Chapter 12 – The Mystic

Most of the citizens of Teshon City lived in ignorance of the old munitions depot that still sat in one of the deep vaults beneath it. Those underground chambers were cut from the bedrock and were some of the first Oselian constructions on the peninsula. During the base's brief heyday, multiple access points allowed military personnel entry to the different storage facilities below. However, after the fall and over the following two centuries, many of the shafts collapsed and the deep chambers were mostly forgotten.

Not only were the people of Teshon City unaware of the old explosives stored in the underground, but also, most folks on the surface did not even know that there was an entire community thriving below the streets. In humanity's family tree, the limb of Shifts contains a separate evolved branch. Specific Shifts, whose powers manifested in physical changes, found safety and a place to call home down in the darkness. Those anomalous and more conspicuous individuals dwelt in the underground.

The deep vaults, where the decrepit weaponry slowly rusted, were cordoned off from those inhabitants who lived beneath the city.

Being around the old ammunition was all part of life down below, and most avoided those lower chambers, but they were not inaccessible.

The explosion created a massive cave-in of one section in the underground, and the collapse resulted in a sinkhole on the surface that swallowed several ramshackle dwellings and the people who lived in them. No one in the city above knew what caused the blast, and it resulted in many deaths.

*

"What the fuck was that?" Dozi exclaimed. She and Agrell were both sitting upright in the darkness.

Ilya moaned and pushed herself up as well. "What happened?" she managed.

Dozi fumbled with her candles and got a few of them lit.

The room around them was still, but there was dust in the air from the quake of the explosion. Several items were knocked over and the contents of a few baskets had spilled onto the floor, but overall, everything in Dozi's home was undamaged.

She jumped up, headed up the stairs to the door, and slipped out of the secret entrance.

"How are you feeling?" Agrell asked Ilya.

"My head," she mumbled, "it feels all wobbly inside. Still feeling the potion." Ilya squinted her eyes shut, winced at a fresh wave of pain, and brought her hands to her side. She doubled over and sucked air through her teeth.

Then Dozi reappeared.

"There's no sign of what caused that noise," she stated, "and a bunch of people are out in the street just walking around aimlessly. Doesn't seem like anyone knows what happened. Everyone's just dazed. It's still dark out there," she added, "not even sunrise yet. Let's all try and get some more sleep before dawn."

She tucked Ilya down, blew out the extra candles, and climbed under the cloak with Agrell.

The remaining hours of the night were uneventful, but the three young women spent them in fitful sleep. They dozed in and out of consciousness until a grey glow began to illuminate Dozi's home. Light seeped down from the hidden doorway above, but she still lit several candles to combat the darkness of her basement chamber.

Dozi rose, headed into her kitchen area, and returned with three cold meat pies. She handed one to Agrell and another to Ilya.

"Let's have a look at your bandages," Dozi said as she took a bite of her breakfast.

Ilya lifted the shirt with a wince. "I never thanked you," she managed between harsh breaths, "both of you," and she looked at Agrell.

"We only wanted to help," Agrell replied in her mousy voice.

Blood seeped through Ilya's gauze in the night, and she needed fresh treatment.

"Okay," Dozi commented, "we have to head back to the mystic's place, and I'd like to do that first thing this morning." She took another bite of food. "Also," she continued, "we need to come up with a story about your injury that doesn't mention you're a Shift. I find it's always helpful with something close to the truth. What about..."

Dozi pondered a moment. "You were out foraging and some hunter mistook your movement for an animal. When they realized what they did, they left you for dead, and then we found you trying to get back to the city."

Both Ilya and Agrell nodded with their mouths full.

Soon the food was gone, and the three slowly headed up the stairs and out into the streets.

The sky was grey.

With Ilya leaning on the crutch and Agrell supporting her other side, they followed Dozi through the Spritehood back toward the mystic's apothecary. After only a few blocks, they came upon a significant commotion.

"What's going on?" Dozi asked a man who tried to run past them towards whatever was happening. She snatched his arm.

He turned on her but not in anger; his expression was one of deep concern. There were dark smears on his cheeks and forehead and hands.

"Didn't you hear it last night?" and his voice cracked as he spoke. "That explosion? The ground collapsed at Three Corners," he declared, "right under some people's houses. All morning we've been trying to find survivors." He noticed Ilya's condition. "Did she get hurt in the explosion?"

Dozi snapped a reply immediately, before either of the other two women could respond. "Yes! That's exactly it! She was hurt because of the explosion and we are taking her someplace safe," she lied.

"Good, take her as far away from the sinkhole as possible. There's no telling if more of the city is going to collapse." The man ran off toward the devastation.

Several blocks later, the three women arrived at the apothecary. The jolly little round man was not alone, and a handsome younger fellow was with him. He was of average height and build, and his complexion was a rich dark brown. He smiled at them as Dozi opened the front door. The man was quite becoming.

"Welcome!" he called out. "Is there something that I can help you find today?"

The mystic interrupted him.

"Welcome back, ladies." The little round man seemed serious. "Let's get you in the back and take a look." When the other fellow realized the mystic already helped the three women, he nodded and returned to whatever task was occupying him before they arrived.

In the back room, Ilya leaned the crutch against the wall, and she sat down on the cushioned table again. She lifted her shirt, and Dozi handed the mystic the clothes he lent to Ilya.

"Fresh bandages," the man stated. He placed the clothes on a shelf and turned to Ilya. "Looks like there's a bit of seepage on the front and quite a bit more from the back. Not to worry, that's to be expected from a wound this severe."

He was not smiling, but he was delicate as he worked. He removed the soiled cloths and applied fresh ointment to the gruesome wounds.

Ilya groaned at the pain and tears leaked from her eyes. The treatment for the damage in her side was necessary, but it was excruciating. However, the little man was soon done, and Ilya began to catch her breath.

The mystic was quick and precise in his ministrations, but he seemed crestfallen. He asked in a gentle voice, "So my dear, do you remember what happened to you? Your friends seemed unsure yesterday."

Ilya looked at Dozi.

"Some hunters shot me," she told the mystic, and added, "accidentally."

"They left her for dead," Dozi interjected. "We found her bleeding and trying to make her way toward the city. I bandaged her up as best I could in the forest. Then we brought her to you. We never met her before yesterday," she added.

He did not seem to be paying much attention to Dozi or Ilya's words.

Then Agrell spoke up and asked him, "Is something wrong?"

The mystic looked at her, and he suddenly threw his arms above his head and wailed, "My little moth! I have no way to check on her!"

All three of the women were caught off-guard, and Agrell replied to him with sympathy in her voice. "What happened? Can we help?"

The door opened and the other man barged into the back room. He wrapped his arms around the mystic.

"Don't tell them anything, honey," he commanded.

The little round man replied to him, "Why not? I need to make sure my baby is okay, and I would accept anyone's assistance in locating her." He pleaded through his tears to the man, "Baby, I need to know that she's alright."

"I know, my love, I know, but we will figure it out ourselves. We don't need strangers to get involved," and his husband held him close as the mystic blubbered into his chest.

"But the explosion," he said through his sobs, "the cave-in, what if she's injured? What if she's dead?" and his shoulders heaved as he cried out in misery.

His man squeezed him tightly and reiterated, "We will figure it out."

Then Ilya spoke up in a quavering voice. "Is she a Bio-Shift?"

The two turned and looked at her with their mouths agape and eyes wide.

"How did you determine that?" the mystic's husband asked.

The mystic replied at the same time. "Yes!" he bawled. "My baby is a Biological Shift, and I'm so worried about her! Part of the city sank, and that can only mean something terrible has happened in the underground," and tears streamed down his face.

Ilya may still have been in pain, but managed to ask through her teeth, "What's her name?"

The two men looked each other in the eye. The mystic nodded to his husband, and the handsome fellow replied.

"Lahari," he said. "She is a beautiful, sensitive child, and when it was revealed that she was a shift, her powers started to change her. The poor girl's entire body is scaled like a reptile, and little spikes stick out from her skin on the sides of her face and down her neck." He continued over the mystic's sobs. "All of the lovely red hair of her childhood fell out, and her skull changed shape. Even her bright brown eyes changed and lightened until they turned yellow."

The mystic stared into the eyes of the man he loved. "Theolan, please, tell them more."

He nodded and continued. "Lahari is still a beautiful girl," Theolan declared, "but early on, she realized that she fit in better with other Biological Shifts in the underground, and we supported her decision to join them. Neither of us can handle going underground. Admittedly, I'm not made for adventures or danger, or even getting dirty, really," he added. "She comes up from time to time and visits with us at night, when it's less likely that someone will see her and be startled by her appearance. We both love her, and we're terribly worried about what's happened in the underground, but neither of us are heroes."

"And you think we are?" Dozi said in an incredulous tone.

"No, no," the mystic replied through his tears, "but we have no one! We lost our friends and family when it turned out Lahari was a Shift and we refused to shun her. I couldn't," he cried, "she's my little moth!"

His husband looked saddened at the mystic's words. "We have each other, my love," Theolan replied, "and we are all we need." He kissed the crying man's forehead.

"Obviously we can't help either," Dozi stated, waving at Ilya. "She can't make it into the underground."

"But I can," Agrell interrupted, and the four others looked at her. She grew sheepish under their gaze, and she repeated a little quieter, "I can." Then she added, "I want to help. Although, I don't know where it is."

"Thank you!" the mystic blubbered.

"No," Dozi declared, "you've been in Teshon for a single day, skinny girl, and now you're just gonna go traipsing through the bowels of the city for..." Dozi paused before letting the word *freak* slip out of her mouth, and went with the common title, "a Bio-Shift?"

Agrell looked at the two men. "If you tell me where to go and how to find her, I'll look through the underground." She turned to Dozi. "You keep calling me *skinny girl*, maybe I'm skinny just for this reason."

Dozi furrowed her brow. "I think what you're thinking of as destiny, is actually genetics, but I guess I can't stop you from being noble." She turned to the mystic and his husband. "Be specific," Dozi demanded. "Give Agrell as much detail as you can manage, and is there some trinket or token, or something important you can give her that she can show your little girl when she finds her?"

"Oh, yes," the mystic's husband exclaimed, "she made me this." Theolan reached for his collar and pulled a thin chord from around his neck. He lifted it over his head and extended the necklace toward Agrell. Attached to the strip of leather was a purple gemstone in a setting of silver.

"Tell her that *her Theolan* and *her ada* is so worried about her!" the mystic wailed.

His husband squeezed him and continued to explain. "Lahari is part of the underground community. Others down there will know who she is, even if they don't know us," and Theolan indicated himself and his husband. "Please, ask about her to anyone you come across."

"Is there anything else I should know about what she looks like?" Agrell asked.

"She's about your height," Theolan replied. "Her skin turned this sort of pale blue-grey hue when her powers kicked in, and then it began developing its scaly quality. The black spines that grew from her face and neck and her yellow eyes were the last physical changes. She's very unique, but among the other underground dwellers, she fits right in."

"I'll do it," Agrell declared. "Show me where the entrance is and I will locate her."

"Help me find our lantern," the mystic said to his husband, and the two men left the little back room.

"This is a bad idea," Dozi stated.

Agrell did not reply.

Ilya added in a weak voice, "His kid is a Shift," and she looked at Dozi. "He gave up the people in his life to have some semblance of a relationship with her."

"I *still* don't fucking trust him," Dozi responded, and she crossed her arms.

Ilya turned to Agrell. "You can't possibly know what you'll encounter in the underground. The people below may not look much like the rest of us, but they are *my* kind. They are Shifts, and they will not like it if they find out you're a Messiah."

"There are a bunch of weirdos who live down there," Dozi mumbled, and she shook her head.

Ilya scrunched up her face at the word. "They can't help it," she said, her brow furrowing. "No Shift asked to be born that way. Even me, I don't have any physical abnormalities, but I still would rather have been born human."

And I wish that I was something more, Dozi thought to herself.

Ilya winced at the pain in her side, and said through gritted teeth, "Also, it's their child, their own daughter who is the Bio-Shift, so watch what you say in front of them." She nodded to the door that the men just exited through, and it opened again as they returned with a small handheld lamp.

"This should help," said the mystic.

"Thank you for doing this," his husband added. "We're so worried about her!"

"Show me where to go," Agrell requested.

"It's not far," the mystic told her, and he and his husband led her out of the back room.

"I don't know," Dozi said to Ilya in a growl. "I just don't trust them."

"If you don't trust them, why did you bring us back here?"

"Because I don't have the means to handle your very fresh and very serious wounds. He's taking care of you."

Ilya looked toward the door. "Why don't you go after them and stay with her."

"Because I definitely don't trust that mystic with you. Besides, as a Messiah, they can't hurt Agrell," Dozi added. "She's brand new to the city, and you're right, there's no telling what she'll encounter in the underground. I was barely aware that there even was an underground to Teshon."

Ilya squinted at another bolt of pain. She sucked air through her teeth and took a quavering breath before she spoke. "You seem to care about others, Dozi," she observed. "I can tell you like to act tough, but you're worried about Agrell."✪

Chapter 13 - Lahari, Part One

The mystic and his husband led Agrell a few blocks to where the land fell into the ocean. She turned her gaze out to the vast expanse of rolling blue beneath the grey sky, and she stared at the sea with wonder. A railing ran along the path above the water's edge, which was only a short drop below them. They stepped up and placed their hands on the rail.

"Her passage is just there," said the mystic, as he leaned over the railing. He pointed down and Agrell could see the lip of a pipe. It was easy to miss, even though he showed her right where to look. "The opening may have been a ventilation shaft. It's too small for most people to use," the mystic added.

"I'm sure I can fit," Agrell responded. Her voice sounded confident. She was keen to help.

Theolan informed her, "There's a chunk of stone that Lahari uses as a step to climb up and down from the rocks below," and he pointed at a small protrusion.

Agrell descended with ease and planted her feet on the rocks that stretched along the water line. She looked back up at the men who were just a little ways above her head, then she peered into the tunnel.

"This may take a while," she stated. "Are you going to wait or go back to your shop?"

"I was too discombobulated before," the mystic replied, "and I'm not sure if I bandaged your friend properly. I also need to make her a fresh potion." Then another sob choked his words, and he said, "Thank you for doing this. All my treatments for her will be on the house."

Agrell did not consider that they would need to pay for his care of Ilya, and his offer felt like a generous bonus for her searching the underground. The men watched from above, as she climbed into the small opening. She crouched and shuffled forward through the narrow concrete tunnel. The pipe was not large and she made her way hunched down.

After a very short distance, she came to a panel that blocked her way. A hinge creaked as she pushed the wall in front of her, and it opened. Agrell stepped out into an underground chamber that was tall enough for her to stand upright. It led only a little ways ahead to a corner, and around it was a door. Agrell opened it and discovered a flight of stone stairs.

She descended, but only a short way down she came to an impasse. It looked like there was a terrible collapse, and she wondered if it was from the explosion the previous night. The walls and ceiling were severely damaged, and the debris filled and blocked her progress down.

Agrell looked at one of the massive chunks of broken masonry in front of her with uncertainty, but she grabbed both sides of it with her hands and lifted. As if it were no more than a pebble, or made of foam, she raised the giant slab of cracked concrete above her head.

"No!" cried the voice of a woman from somewhere unseen. "Put it back!

Agrell looked around but could not tell where the voice came from or who was speaking.

"What are you doing in my tunnel?"

Agrell stood there holding the huge stone, feeling surprised and unsure, and she replied, "I'm trying to find someone after the explosion."

"Humans aren't welcome in the underground," the voice declared. "Go back the way you came, and do not return. There's no one down here for you."

Agrell put the stone down and called out, "I need to find someone's daughter."

"We who dwell below no longer hold ties to those on the surface. In the light is no place for those such as we. Be gone!"

"I think her name's Lahari!" Agrell said over the woman's voice.

Then there was silence.

Agrell decided to speak up again. "Do you know anyone by that name, Lahari? Or maybe something close to it?"

She received no reply.

Agrell tried to explain. "There was an explosion last night in the underground. You must be aware of what happened. There's a mystic up here who says his daughter lives below, and he is so worried about her. I think she's just a child. He calls her his little moth."

The voice spoke, but now it was quiet. "Ada?" it said.

Agrell did not understand, and asked again, "Do you know someone named Lahari, or maybe Lahara, or Lahira?"

Scraping noises that sounded like stone against stone started coming from the debris in front of her. The pieces began shifting, and a moment later a monstrous young woman stepped out of the rubble, but it remained in place behind her.

"Ada?" she said again.

Agrell's eyes opened very wide, and her jaw dropped. She took a step back from the woman and held up the necklace with its purple gemstone.

No descriptions from the mystic or his husband could have prepared Agrell for the inhuman person who stood before her. She was not a little girl.

Agrell did not even consider that the woman was naked, because her skin was an unnatural bluish color that was lighter on her face, and much darker over the rest of her body. Almost every inch of her bizarre epidermis was covered in small plate scales that were each about the size of a coin. Her skull was ridged with a trio of crests that rose from her bald scaly head. Coupled with her skin, she looked very reptilian. Black quills like those of a sea urchin stuck out all around her face like countless tiny horns. They also protruded from the sides and back of her neck, and they got larger the farther down they grew. More spines stabbed out from her shoulders and upper arms, as well as from her hips and the sides of her thighs.

She stared at Agrell with sparkling golden eyes, took a step forward, and reached out to take the handmade piece of jewelry.

"Ada sent you?" the woman asked. "He's never told anyone about my secret passage."

"Ada?" Agrell repeated. "Is that your father? Are you Lahari?"

Lahari nodded. "I am."

"He's worried about you, both of your fathers are. Someone that I know is hurt and they are helping her. Then there was the explosion last night, and they were so worried about you today, so I offered to come find you because I could fit through the tunnel that you use when you visit them."

Agrell could not determine what the expression on Lahari's strange face meant.

"I just wanted to help," Agrell reiterated. "Why don't you come up with me and tell them you're okay? I know that would make them feel better."

"Why don't *you* just tell them I'm fine," Lahari countered. She looked up at the ceiling. "It's daytime, I can't go out there now anyway."

Agrell did not know how Lahari made that deduction from within the darkness of the basement chamber, but she was correct that the sun was up.

"Please," Agrell began, but Lahari interrupted her.

"It's not safe for my kind to go above ground during the day. We attract too much attention to ourselves, and that's a bad thing. Just tell my dads that you found me and I'm unharmed. They will understand. Now, go," she commanded. "You can't be found down here by the others." She turned her back on Agrell. The scales were larger and darker along her spine and on her shoulder blades.

Agrell watched but did not comprehend how Lahari walked through the rubble. The boulders just seemed to move out of her way and reposition themselves behind her. Then Agrell was alone again. She climbed the stairs to the door and entered the chamber beyond, but when she arrived, she found a bare wall. There was no opening to the tunnel that led outside.

The wall kept its secrets hidden, and Agrell brought her hands to it. She felt all over the surface in front of her, but the wall was solid. She was perplexed; she knew that she came in through there, and Lahari told her to go back out the same way, but there was no exit.

Agrell considered that she probably possessed the ability to punch her way through, but she was still unfamiliar with her enhancements. She did not know what the wall supported and was certain that destroying it would attract unwanted attention. She knew that she just needed to figure out its secret, and she stepped back for a better look at the entire wall. Then the door to the stairs opened and banged into her.

Lahari popped her head out to see why the door did not open all the way, and she was startled by the sight of Agrell.

"What are you still doing here? I told you to leave."

"I can't find the exit."

Lahari looked at the wall as she came through the doorway.

"Oh, right, it's a secret," she stated and stepped up with Agrell behind her. She pointed toward the floor and used her toes to push against a tiny panel on the wall. The hidden door opened to reveal the tunnel.

Agrell stepped into it and shuffled through again in her crouched position. The glow at the end seemed bright to her, even with the gray cloud cover dimming the already pale winter sun. She popped out, stepped onto the rocks at the water's edge, and put one foot onto the stone that jutted out from the wall. Agrell pulled herself up to the edge of the footpath and peered both directions. No one was coming, and she climbed all the way up.

"Coast is clear," Agrell whispered down.

Lahari stuck her very unique head out of the tunnel and looked up at Agrell. "I can't go out there. I already told you that. Tell my fathers I'm here, and they will know what to do."

"Wait a second," Agrell said, "why did you come up the stairs? I mean, I know that I was stuck and couldn't find the exit in there, but why did you follow me?"

"The explosion," Lahari explained, "it didn't seem as bad in my area of the underground, but I was wrong. Those stairs lead deep under Teshon City, and they are my secret way up to the surface and back down again, but near the bottom, there's an extensive cave-in and the damage is extreme."

"You couldn't get through?" Agrell asked.

Lahari looked at her with another expression Agrell could not decipher. "Right," she answered.

She did not say anything else and Agrell replied, "I'll go get your dads."

Lahari's head disappeared back into the tunnel.

Agrell then realized that she was unsure how to get back to the apothecary. It was only a few blocks away from the coast, but she did not know which direction to go. She did not remember walking along the path above the water, so she took the nearest street that led straight into the neighborhood. After a short distance, she came to a sign for an apothecary and headed toward it. She pulled open the door, but it looked very different inside, and a woman greeted her.

"Hello, what can I get you?"

"I'm just looking for someone!" Agrell blurted out in reply before closing the door.

She looked around at the nearby shops. There were two other mystics' storefronts in view, and Agrell was frustrated with herself that she did not know where she was going. She peered in through several windows, but none of the interiors seemed familiar, and she checked down a couple of side streets that revealed still more apothecaries and herb shops. Agrell did not remember turning with the mystic and his husband, so she decided not to venture down any of them.

"Hey, skinny girl!"

Agrell was relieved to hear the voice of someone she knew, and she turned.

Dozi was standing in front of the entrance to the shop.

"I found her!" Agrell cried out, but her hand shot up to her mouth.

Dozi chuckled to herself and shook her head.

They entered the shop and Agrell repeated herself in a quieter voice.

"I found her. I found Lahari!"

The two men looked relieved as if a terrible weight were removed from their shoulders. The mystic started to cry again, and his husband's face broke into an enthusiastic smile.

"She is waiting for you at the tunnel," Agrell continued. "She said she can't come up in the light, but she also can't get back into the rest of the underground. Her passage is blocked."

"I am just so glad she's okay," blubbered Lahari's father.

His husband was beaming. "Thank you, thank you," he kept repeating.

"Nice work, skinny girl," Dozi added★

Chapter 14 - Underground, Part One

With fresh bandages on Ilya's face and side, the three women left the mystic's shop and made their way back to Dozi's hidden home. One after another, they slipped inside behind the fan cage and descended into her chamber.

It was much colder down below than it was that morning when they left.

"What happened?" Agrell asked.

"Why is it freezing down here?" Dozi added.

They reached the bottom of the stairs and Ilya leaned on her crutch. She raised her free arm. "It's there," she told the other two, and she pointed toward one of the gaps that led into another part of the basement.

Dozi slipped into the crawlspace and disappeared. "I can't feel any difference," she called behind her. "It's just cold."

Ilya reiterated. "No, it's coming from there. I can feel something different in the air."

"What does that mean?" Dozi yelled back. She stepped out into an open area that she used to store things. "I don't see anything, I can't tell why it's cold."

"Does that part go farther?" Agrell called to her.

"I mean," Dozi replied, "it does, but there's just some old ducting."

"Maybe I can fit through," Agrell called out to her. She did not await a reply and also slipped through the gap and followed Dozi.

"Hey, skinny girl," Dozi said as Agrell emerged. "It's right there, but I don't feel comfortable crawling through it." She pointed and peered into the narrow space that led deeper into the bowels beneath the rundown military buildings above.

Agrell called back to Ilya, "I think I can fit through. I'll see where the cold is coming from."

"How does she know the cold is from here? And why is it so fucking freezing?" Dozi pulled her bulky clothes tighter and shivered. "Well, go on, I guess," she said to Agrell and waved toward the small opening. Dozi then added, "Be careful!"

For quite a way, the passage only provided Agrell space to crawl, but she eventually emerged into a gap between two rusted metal walls. They seemed to be part of something larger, but she could not tell much about the old military equipment from where she was. The space between them led her to the reason it was so cold.

A pale glow was coming from one side, and at first, Agrell was not sure what she was seeing, but then there could be no doubt; light was somehow making its way to the underground chamber. She approached a huge section of collapsed masonry and broken bedrock. Light was seeping in, but the pathetic glow did less to illuminate anything in the darkness than it did to simply draw her attention.

The scrawny young woman began moving one massive piece of stone after another. It felt so unnatural for her to be this strong, but it allowed her to discover the source of the cold.

The cave-in seemed precarious and Agrell did not want to cause another collapse. Once there was space, she squeezed through toward the opening where the gray glow was making its way inside. With it came the frigid winter air from outside.

Agrell headed back in the opposite direction and was surprised to find a hidden fissure in the darkness. A massive crack in the stone led down deeper into the earth. She was curious about the opening in the bedrock and wriggled her way into the tight space. At some parts, she needed to squat down and shimmy under lower regions where the ceiling was right above her head, but Agrell managed not to get stuck and eventually came to a void at the end of the crack. She poked her head out and looked down.

The opening was in the wall of a stairwell. Upwards was blocked by much more fallen rubble, but the stairs below were clear. She climbed down from the hole and began to descend into the depths beneath Teshon City. Before reaching the bottom, Agrell saw a light and heard voices, and she paused. The stairs led to a hallway, and the talking was coming from a chamber that opened in one side of it. Agrell peeked around the door's frame.

Three unique people were toiling together, and Agrell tried to understand them in terms that made sense to her.

One of them appeared to be a skinny woman covered in feathers. She seemed to be naked and all of her exposed skin was accented with little strange curls that fluttered as she moved.

There was a second woman, and the only word Agrell needed to use that encompassed her was *giant*. She was abnormally huge, towering over the bird woman, with arms and legs the size of a normal person's waist. The giantess wore a patchwork outfit that was clearly made to accommodate her size.

Their third companion was a bald man wearing only a pair of underwear. His skin was an unnatural shade of green, not sickly, but almost plantlike. However, his primary peculiarity was that tiny crackles of electricity appeared to be sparking from his entire epidermis. The shocks traveled over the man's green skin, running up and down his limbs, and over his face and head and torso.

The three of them were carrying large objects wrapped in sheets, and Agrell was disturbed by the look of the things. One by one, the rigid forms under their pale shrouds were dropped into a stone well at the center of the room. Smoke was issuing from its mouth that coiled up to a chimney in the ceiling. Despite being deep underground, any fumes were syphoned away and the room was not hazy.

"What's the count up to?" growled the giantess.

"Who knows at this point," replied the green electric man. "Let's get the next group."

They dropped the last of the wrapped objects into the well and began to approach the door where Agrell was hiding.

She turned in surprise and jumped. To her further surprise, her jump launched her all the way up to where the stairs were blocked. She soared high, landed against the fallen rubble, and she clung to the rocks above like a bat.

The giantess ducked through the doorway and entered the hall followed by the other two, but to Agrell's relief, they turned their backs on her and headed down the corridor in the opposite direction of the stairs. When they were gone, she let go of the wall and fell hard, but she landed upright on her feet.

She raced back down the steps, entered the room, and approached the well. Over its edge, she saw the churning orange glow of liquid magma. Whatever was dropped down the well was now gone. The rest of the room was empty. She returned to the hall and proceeded to the next room. It opened to yet another set of stairs that led farther under the earth.

"Another 17," growled a voice. It came from below.

Agrell turned and sprinted back up to the stairs and hid in the darkness.

The three figures returned, and the giantess' arms were loaded with more sheet-wrapped objects. As they reentered the room with the well, Agrell crept back down to the doorway.

"We've lost so many," the bird woman said in a voice filled with sorrow. "Who else did you hear about?" she asked the electric man.

The giantess grunted and lowered her burden to the floor. They continued to drop the things down to the fiery depths.

"Both of the stone brothers died," the man replied. "Three of the werefolk are dead. There's an entire group from the netherswamp missing, and let's not forget that ground zero was in the lab, so the angel and demon plus anyone who was in purgatory is just gone, just fucking gone."

"I overheard someone saying that the astral cave collapsed," the giantess added in despair.

"The submerged tunnel no longer exists," the green electric man continued. "There is a crack in the hypron chamber, and no one has been able to reach..."

Agrell was silent, but then the bird woman suddenly spoke over her companions.

"There's someone else down here," she said, and the three looked toward the door✪

Chapter 15 - Hunters

Talin stepped up in front of his superiors, lowered down to one knee, and bowed his head. The huge desk behind which they all sat loomed over him.

"Did you get the gland?" one of them asked.

Talin held up a small jar, and other leaders began speaking.

"Call the grand hierophant!"

"Bring the next group of unborn!"

"Gather the ingredients for the spell!"

"What do you suppose the next generation will be granted?"

One of the attendants took the jar from Talin. He rose and stepped to the side of the chamber with the other members of his crew. None of them said a word.

Their base of operations was in a huge old warehouse in the middle of the industrial district. Its interior was cordoned off into several separate sections. Within the leadership area, the desk was the primary focus, and a faded Oselian rug stretched out on the ground before it. At the opposite end of the warehouse, the chapel of Demifae stood empty, but soon it would be full.

One of the women leaders stood and leaned forward with her palms on the desk. "Our hunts have become more successful of late, and we propose ordering several groups out at once. What say you?" she asked those gathered, and she received resounding *Ayes*!

"Talin," she continued, turning to the man, "are you and your crew in need of a rest, or can we expect you to move on to your next target." Her words were not a question.

"No, milady," he replied, "my squad don't need a rest, and we can push the timetable up to whenever you command."

"Very good," his leader responded. She then added with a scowl, "I still hate your team's fucking name." She gave orders to a few other crew leaders, and then the meeting was adjourned.

Talin and his team headed to their quarters in the rundown Oselian barracks. He slammed their door closed.

"That old toad!" he raged. "She's never satisfied, and she will never be. We are down a crewmember, and not a word of mention was given for him, only if we are too tired for another hunt. A hunt, might I add, which is not properly planned! All of us lost one of our own, a Demifae, and they didn't acknowledge him."

"Fuck her," Claw Two added.

"And furthermore," Talin spat, "we should be at the spell-casting with the gland we procured!"

"Let's just fucking get this over with," Claw Four stated. "Our next Shift's routine isn't hammered down yet," he continued, "and Claw Three did some of the surveillance, so any insights were taken with him to the grave."

"What do we know?" Talin asked him.

"This particular Shift can manifest or summon entities of some sort," Claw Four told the others. "We have not determined the full extent of its powers, but Claw Three informed me that he was confident there would be nothing out of the ordinary when it was time for the next hunt."

"Fine!" snapped Talin. "Gear up, and let's find this Shift. We don't know where it will be or how soon we'll be able to corner it and take it out." He growled to himself, "So fucking unprepared."

Talin's own elevation to Demifae was a mere four years prior, but he soon ascended the ranks of hunters and was given command of his own pack. The spell that was cast over the group in which Talin was a member gained him the gift of farther-vision. He hoped for something more active or aggressive; super-sight was not high on his list of desired powers.

Claw Two could generate venom like a snake. Claw Four was a regenerator who possessed the ability to heal himself quickly. Even Claws One and Three possessed different versions of an ability that allowed them to suck the lifeforce from their enemies. Similar to their leader, Claws Five and Six both were gifted with a heightened sense, but they each gained ultra-hearing from the spells that elevated them above humans. Claw Seven's enhancement was the most like Talin's, but instead of seeing far, it was the ability to see at night.

The loss of Claw Three was a major blow to Talin's Talons.

"Before we head back out, we remember our fallen soldier," Talon declared to the others.

He poured seven shots of whistlewhiskey, and they each knocked them back. The group shared a quiet moment before anyone spoke again, and it was their leader's voice that broke the silence.

"There was a book," Talon began to say.

"Here we go again," commented Claw Six with a smirk.

"Every time," added Claw One.

"He can't help himself," said Claw Seven.

"Has he even read it?" asked Claw Two to the others with a chuckle.

Claws Four and Five remained silent.

"There was a book," Talon repeated over his crew's sarcasm, "that described the act of hunting those such as us, or us as we used to be. But now we, fellow hunters, we hunt something far more deadly, far more elusive and vicious than mere humans. We are hunting demons, devils in a world where they don't belong."

"Death to all monsters!" declared Claw Five.

"We hunt to stop the spread," Talin continued. "We hunt to raise humanity. We hunt the enemies of life."

"Death to all monsters!" the Claws proclaimed in unison.

Talin concluded, "We are monster hunters!" ★

Chapter 16 - Underground, Part Two

In the chamber with the well of magma, the bird-like woman approached the door, as Agrell raced up the stairs. Without being seen, she slipped into the crack of the wall. She shimmied back a few paces from the stairwell, and paused.

"Oi, you lot!" a new voice called from farther down the hallway.

Agrell peeked out as the bird woman stepped toward the approaching figure.

It was a person with four arms.

Agrell could not determine much else about the individual. Their voice was commanding.

The bird woman spoke. "We're nearly done with these." She turned and re-entered the room with the well.

The four-armed figure followed.

Agrell decided that she had lingered long enough, and she wriggled her way through the fissure in the bedrock until she could again see the gray glow where the crack opened to the outside. She continued and crawled back into the open area of Dozi's home to inform the other two women what she found.

"Is there any way to patch the hole and keep the cold out?" Dozi asked, more to herself than the other two.

Ilya asked her own question. "What were they dropping down the well?"

None of them spoke for a moment. Agrell's description did not include the word *bodies*, but Dozi and Ilya were thinking that.

Dozi then asked, "Is Teshon City built on a volcano?"

"The peninsula is part of the lowlands," Ilya stated. "The mountains are much farther inland. Does it make sense that there is a volcano under the city?"

"What about the people down there finding the crack and coming up here into your home?" Agrell asked.

"There's nothing we can do about that right now," Dozi replied. "Sounds like even you could barely slither through, skinny girl, so let's not worry about anyone below unless we need to. And I don't think you should go back down there again. No telling what would happen if a group of them found you."

"I agree," added Ilya. "I understand that you became a Messiah against your will, but many of the city's citizens will not see beyond that."

Agrell dropped her head in shame.

"Not your fault, skinny girl," Dozi said in a surprisingly kind voice. She glanced at the light that seeped in from above. "Sundown is on its way," she informed them. "There's nothing we can do to deal with the cold tonight, other than sleeping all bundled up." Dozi kept to herself the crushing disappointment that she felt about her home being damaged and potentially becoming unlivable.

"Let's get some food in us and try to sleep," she added. "I've still got a few meat pies left." As she headed into her kitchen area, she mumbled to herself. "These things were supposed to last me a week."

After the three ate, Dozi situated Ilya on her bed.

"I don't need a blanket," Ilya informed her. "My powers make it so I'm not affected by the cold, and you both should have all the covers."

"Really?" Agrell asked. Her eyes were filled with wonder, but Ilya shared no more about it.

Instead of disrobing like the previous night, Dozi added extra clothes to her already bundled body and swapped the beanie she was wearing for a thicker knit cap that she pulled down over her ears. She also handed Agrell a heavy sweater and hat, then she pointed her toward the pile of blankets.

After Dozi prepared Ilya's potion, she got down beside Agrell, and the two curled up together. Despite the cold, they soon fell asleep in the darkness✪

Chapter 17 - Lahari, Part Two

The next morning, while the three women were getting ready to head back to the mystic's, a spark of inspiration struck Agrell.

"Maybe Lahari can use the crack in the bedrock that now leads to the underground, as a passage up to see her dads. Since her hidden path is blocked, she's stuck in the stairwell and doesn't have any way back down to be with her people."

"Do you even think she could fit?" Ilya asked.

"Whoa, whoa!" Dozi interjected. "We will not be offering my home to be used by a monster from the underground as a thoroughfare!"

"*Hey!*" snapped Ilya with a scowl. "Don't say that!"

"Yeah," Agrell agreed, "Lahari is not a monster."

"You both know what I mean!" Dozi retorted, and she plowed on. "I've already opened my home to both of you, with the understanding that it's secret. No one besides you two knows about this place, and I don't want anyone else privy to it, especially not some Bio-Shift child from the underground!"

"She's not a child," Agrell responded. "She's an adult."

"*Even better!*" Dozi barked, her voice thick with sarcasm. "A full-grown Bio-Shift, with who knows what powers! You think I want them sneaking through my home in the middle of the night?"

Dozi stormed into her kitchen, and the other two women could hear her banging around in the cupboards.

"Ugh!" she exclaimed from the other room. "*Fine.*" Dozi returned with two meat pies. Her shoulders were drooped and she was frowning. "Fine," she repeated.

"You're going to let her use your home to see her dads?" Agrell asked.

"*Yes!*" Dozi said dramatically, and she rolled her eyes. "We can tell the three of them about my home, I guess. I know you're both right," she conceded before either of them could say anything else. "Yes," she repeated, "we can tell the mystic that his daughter can return to the underground through my home."

She changed subjects.

"These are my last meat pies. Skinny girl, you and I can split one and we'll grab something else on the street, or maybe from the mystic when we head back to get you patched up again," and Dozi nodded to Ilya as she handed her one of the pies.

When she and Agrell finished their shared meal, Ilya offered some of what was left of hers, but both insisted she should finish it.

"Might not find something as substantial out in the city," Dozi said, "and you need the energy for recovery."

Soon the three women were out in the grey light again. They made their way through the Spritehood at Ilya's slower pace, but before long, they arrived at the mystic's apothecary.

"We found a way to get Lahari back to the underground!" Agrell declared as they entered.

Dozi told the mystic and his husband what happened in the lower part of her basement home, and Agrell explained in detail what she saw below. Dozi was a little reluctant but shared with the men the location of her hidden door behind the old fan cage.

"Oh, I don't know how to thank you," the mystic said, with tears flowing down his round cheeks. He took her hands in his and proclaimed, "Your generosity is boundless!"

Dozi was surprised by the action, as he bounced in place with his enthusiasm.

"You've been caring for Ilya," he continued, "and now you're going to share your home, so that my little moth can still come up to see her daddies. You are so kind!"

"Yes, yes," Dozi confirmed. She gripped his hands and pulled him from the backroom. The two of them stepped into the front of his empty shop.

When they were alone, he asked her, "What is it, my dear?"

"I want to be a Demifae," she declared. "If your girl is gonna sneak through my house, I want to be made a Demifae in exchange."

The mystic looked horrified and pulled his hands from hers.

Theolan popped through the door behind them and saw the expression on his husband's face.

"What's wrong?" he asked. "What happened?"

"I want to be more than I am," Dozi replied to him, and she repeated herself. "I want to be a Demifae."

Now the mystic's husband looked appalled. *"How could you ask something like that?"* he snapped at her.

Dozi was taken aback. She scowled at them. "What's the fucking deal with you two?" she barked in reply. "You're already a Demifae," she proclaimed to the mystic. "This is what you do, isn't it? I just want to be more than a human, and I won't be denied," she added.

"Oh, honey," the mystic said, and his tone softened, "I don't do that anymore."

Both the men became more gentle, and Theolan hugged his husband close, as the mystic explained.

"When my own precious, brilliant, young daughter began to change," he said in a calm voice, "I suddenly realized that what I was doing was so terribly wrong. I have not practiced my trained *arts*," and he said the word with disdain, "since my little moth began to change. Lahari opened my eyes, revealed to me the error of my ways. Shifts are people, Dozi," he continued, and his voice was full of compassion.

"I have not used a photonova gland for any purpose in almost a decade. No, I'm sorry, my new dear friend," he said, as he took her hands again. "I cannot make you a Demifae, and if I could go back with the things that I now feel, I would not have been part of the spell that made me one. A person, someone's child, someone's beautiful child was murdered for the enchantment, and all I am now able to do is hold my breath for a long time. That's it; all I can do is hold my breath. Is that worth the poor Shift's life?"

The mystic stared into Dozi's eyes. "There are people out there right now," he went on, "who want to kill Shifts for their photonova glands. There are people who would murder my beautiful, incredible, powerful daughter, and then cannibalize the very part of her physical body that makes her so unique."

He squeezed Dozi's hand. "I can't change your mind for you, but please reconsider your intention to become a Demifae. Every Shift was someone's baby. I realize that not every child is loved, and it's very common for Shifts to be ostracized or disowned by their families when their abilities are revealed," he paused, "but would you murder someone, Dozi? Could you take the life of another, and all for a measly power like mine? Is that worth it?"

Dozi did not say anything. The mystic's words felt like truths she never considered before, but it was almost as if she had been waiting to be told all the things he said. These new ideals clashed with the desires that lingered in her heart. She felt conflicted, as she returned to the back room with the two men.

"I want to go tell Lahari the good news!" Agrell declared as they entered.

The mystic's face broke into a beaming smile. "You are our heroine!" he proclaimed.

Dozi's frustration with herself came out, and she turned it on the mystic. "Don't call her that!" she snapped. "As if she's not quite a *hero* because she's a woman. Diminishing her willingness to try and save your daughter is disgraceful." She shot the men a disgusted expression and turned to Agrell. "You're a hero, skinny girl."

The mystic brought his hands to his mouth in shock, and he squawked in an apologetic tone through his fingers, "I didn't mean it like that at all!" He looked from one person to the next. "And in fact, I do believe you're correct," he added, turning back to Dozi. "I've never loved the word heroine," he declared, "and you've just given me an explanation for why I'm allowed to hate it. Thank you for enlightening me!" He seemed delighted, bowed to her, and then corrected himself. "Agrell, you are our hero!"

"Why don't Agrell and I go to see Lahari and tell her about the access to the underground in Dozi's basement," Theolan recommended, "and you can patch up your patient here." He smiled at Ilya, and he kissed his husband.

"Thank you, Agrell," the mystic said with his eyes shimmering as he tried to hold back his tears of joy.

As Theolan and Agrell headed out into the grey day and made their way toward the water's edge, she said, "I kind of expected Lahari to come home to you two last night when it was dark. You haven't seen her?"

"No, she didn't visit us, and I wish our place could *be* her home," he said with regret in his voice. "I absolutely adore her, but she's just not safe in the city."

"It seems strange that she didn't come see you two last night," Agrell wondered, as they stepped up to the railing above the tunnel.

"This time, I'll stick around," Theolan stated, "so you don't get lost again."

She climbed down, crawled through the tunnel, and pushed the hinged door that kept access to the outside a secret. Lahari was on the other side of it. Again, Agrell found the young woman's unique appearance both incredible and frightening. She did her best not to stare and informed Lahari about Dozi's home and the new subterranean crack that led into the Biological Shift underground.

Lahari asked, "Why are you helping me?"

"Isn't that what we're supposed to do," Agrell replied, "help the people we can help?"

"But why did you risk your life for me? You abovelanders are often killed if you're caught in the underground. Don't you know how dangerous it can be for someone like you?"

"I just wanted you to be able to see your dads."

"I don't think you understand," Lahari stated. "You need to stay out of the underground. If those Bio-Shifts you saw at the well caught you, *you'd have been killed*," she reiterated. "Listen to me. If I wasn't alone when we met, you would have been killed. If I was with anyone else when I found you, you'd probably be dead now."

"You mean when *I* found *you*?" Agrell asked.

Lahari looked at her, but the black quills around her pale blue face made her expressions indecipherable.

Agrell added, "I wanted to find you another way between the city and the underground."

"But why are you helping me?" Lahari implored. "I'm a *monster*, according to most abovelanders. I was 13 when my powers began to develop, and that was also when my body started to change. Kids used to call me *dragon skin, grey girl, the ugly urchin*." She stared at Agrell with her sparkling yellow eyes. "You look like every person who ever talked shit to me, insulted me or called me names, and you *normal* people can be cruel, vicious. I was immediately accepted into the underground with my fellow changed Shifts."

"I'm glad you were able to find a new home," Agrell replied in a conciliatory tone.

"I should be allowed on the surface!" snapped Lahari. "I should feel safe walking the streets. I should be allowed to visit my fathers anytime I want, day or night."

"I'm so sorry that things are this way," Agrell said. "I didn't know it was like this. I did not even know there was an entire community underground when I got to the city two days ago."

There was a pause in their conversation.

"Two days?"

"Yes," Agrell confirmed, "I just arrived two days ago after I ran aw..." but she caught herself, and her voice fell silent.

"Ran aw... ay?" Lahari finished for her. "Ran away from what?"

Agrell did not reply.

"Go on. Tell me," urged Lahari.

Agrell sighed. "My family," she whispered.

Lahari let out a wry laugh. "So, you're one, too?"

"One what?"

"You're an outcast," Lahari declared, "but at least you look like a *person*. You didn't have to join us freaks belowground."

Agrell could feel her positive spirit waning. "Don't call yourself that," she said in a quiet voice. "I don't think you're a freak. Would you tell me," she asked Lahari, "what happened with your family when you changed?"

Lahari clicked her tongue. "My dads are both good enough, but my mother is a piece of shit. A lot of the folks down here have shitty families."

She continued. "When I was 13, my mother tried to scrape off my changing scaly skin with a serrated knife. That didn't work, so she started whipping me with a piece of thin chain that she heated in a fire. My ada was already with Theolan at that point, and when they learned everything about my change and how my mother was torturing me, they killed her and dumped her body in the Grey Shallows."

Agrell was more than a little startled by this admission.

Lahari asked, "What about your parents? What'd they do to you?"

Agrell wanted to tell Lahari how sorry she felt for the abuse she suffered. She wanted to let her know that her fathers were each *twice* the parent her mother had been. Agrell even wanted to say that it sounded like Lahari's mother got what she deserved.

All she mumbled in reply was, "I'm not supposed to talk about it." Dozi's warning to refrain from sharing information about her past was fresh in her mind.

"Keeping secrets doesn't make friends," Lahari commented. "Really though, you and I can't possibly be friends. Maybe we can be acquaintances, though. That only works if you share." Lahari then asked, "Do you think there is a single thing that you and your skinny, pretty, normal-looking self has gone through that is even remotely close to what it's like being a Biological Shift? You can go anywhere you want at any time of day or night. No one looks twice at you. You're boring and common, just like everyone else up there."

Agrell decided that Lahari's argument made sense, and instead of following Dozi's advice, she wanted to connect with Lahari and tell her about herself. "I'm from the Lovegood community," she stated.

Lahari's tone changed. "Another escapee, good for you." She sounded impressed. "Well, I'd say your story is more than just that you ran away from your family; you got away from Messiahs."

Lahari's first words stuck in Agrell's mind.

"Another?"

"Yeah," Lahari confirmed, "we've got a few ex-cult members down here, and Auntie Peg is from there too. She's got a shop near my father's apothecary."

"What does that mean? People keep using that word," Agrell said. "I don't even know what it is."

"I'm just saying that you're not the only one who's ever left the Lovegoods."

"N-no," Agrell stuttered, "th-that's not pos-possible."

"Well, now I don't know what *you* mean," Lahari replied. "You're not the only one who's left the Lovegood cult."

Agrell was more shocked by this information, than most other things that she experienced in her few days of freedom. She needed clarification.

"Other people have left the community before me?" she asked, and she made a deduction. "They lied to me?" Agrell whispered, more to herself than the other woman.

Lahari took a breath to ponder the details she was learning about Agrell. "How did you escape?" she asked, and her voice was gentle.

Dozi's recommendation prickled in Agrell's mind, but she now stated conclusively, "I ran away. I didn't know some of the secret things about the community where I grew up, until very recently, and then I felt like they were not who I always thought they were. I couldn't be a part of them anymore. They kept so much hidden," she added in a tone of disbelief.

Lahari remained quiet, and her yellow eyes were fixed on Agrell, who continued.

"I feel like I was inadvertently part of horrible things." Her voice broke, and she choked down a sob. "I feel responsible for the actions taken by my community, and I want to make a difference. I want to make up just a little for the bad things they do."

There was another pause before Lahari asked, "What was it like growing up?"

"Structured!" Agrell blurted out. "I mean, every minute of every day was accounted for, there were obligations we needed to fulfill daily. Everyone in the community needed to be fed, our farm needed tending, and every day there were..." but Agrell's voice faded.

Her little cousin's corpse was barely cold in the ground, if they even buried the poor child's body. He was dead only a matter of days, and sorrow was still burning in Agrell's heart from the ritual.

"There were group things we needed to do every day," she said quietly, but she said no more about it.

Then Lahari asked in a soft voice, "Do they do things to girls?"

Agrell did not understand the question. "What do you mean? Everyone is made to work hard."

"No, that's not what I'm talking about. How do I put this delicately?" Lahari was feeling more compassionate than she expected about the abovelander, and she elaborated. "Was there ever anything that involved you being naked, or a man being naked with you?"

Agrell was stunned by the question. "No! Modesty is a pivotal foundation of our community. Everyone wears the same clothes and does their hair the same way. Being," and she whispered the word, "*naked* was against the rules."

"So you're telling me that they are not doing weird sex shit to kids?"

Agrell paused, attempting to understand this strange line of questioning. "I don't think so," she said in a meek voice.

Lahari tilted her head to one side. "You were never part of any sort of naked ritual or anything?"

Agrell took a sharp breath. "There was nothing like that."

Lahari's expression was unreadable. "You've already realized that they lied to you, in what sounds like a major way. What other things are going on up there unchecked?"

"They killed my little cousin," Agrell whispered. "I guess he was a Shift. He was just a little boy," and she started to cry. "Then I ran away." Even through her tears, she thought it better to keep the details of the ritual to herself.

When her sadness subsided, Agrell apologized. "I'm sorry. It's all still so fresh in my mind." She wiped away her tears.

"They just did this, didn't they?" Lahari asked gently.

Agrell nodded. "Please don't tell anyone where I'm from," she pleaded. "I don't think that's good information to get out."

"I understand, and I think that's wise," Lahari agreed.

Agrell decided to focus on their immediate situation. "Do you know about that underground well with magma below it?"

"I do," Lahari replied. "It's actually at the bottom of my stairs, where the cave-in is most severe. The well is directly under the Messiah Tower, but very deep beneath the earth."

"Do you think that you will be able to use that crack in the rocks in Dozi's home to go back and forth between the underground and seeing your dads?" Agrell asked.

"That all depends, if it's hidden, it may suffice. This passageway," and Lahari waved her blue scaly hands at the hall that led to the stairs, "has been very convenient because it is indeed hidden from you abovelanders, but also, none of my fellow Bio-Shifts know about it. I suspect it's just a matter of time before someone finds that major crack in the bedrock and fixes it." Lahari paused. "Or more likely, we post sentries at it to guard people against entering the underground. Some belowgrounders desire for all of us to sever ties with anyone on the surface."

"Well, that seems extreme."

"Coming from an ex-cult member," Lahari said with a spiny-faced smirk, "that's a very serious criticism, and I happen to agree with you."

"Why do people keep using that word?"

"Which word?" Lahari asked.

"*Cult*," Agrell replied, testing the word for the first time. "Everyone keeps saying the community is a cult, but I don't even know what that word means."

"It's kind of difficult to define," Lahari began. "The term applies to lots of groups who hold extreme beliefs and insist their members do the same. Those people that I just mentioned who want us all down here to pretend that the world above doesn't exist, they're kind of a cult. Let me ask you, were you close with your family?"

Agrell furrowed her brow. "We put more focus..." she started, but she paused and corrected herself. "*They* put more focus into being part of the community, than about families. My mother was always around," she added in a dejected tone.

"Unpleasant lady?" Lahari asked. "What about your father?"

"There was only one man we called *father*, and everyone called him that. I don't think he was my real father; actually, I'm not sure who my father is."

"I knew it," Lahari declared. She ran her fingers over the spines on one side of her face and sighed. "There's some freaky sex shit happening there, I'm sure of it."

Agrell took a breath. "The more people I talk to, the more I realize how little I understand," she conceded, and she continued. "Everyone lives together. Everyone calls everyone else *cousin* if they are close in age, or *elder* if they are older. And we all called our leader father. It was never impressed upon us with any importance that we should know who our biological fathers were; he was our father." Agrell felt like she was divulging too much information, and decided to try and change subjects.

"What was in those bundles the others were dropping down the well?"

Lahari did not hesitate to reply. "Our dead," she declared. "As a community, we decided long ago to remove the opportunity for anyone to find our corpses and steal our mantis glands. You may not know this, but a fully developed mantis gland does not decompose, so even when our bones are dust, the crystalline gland remains. By dropping our dead into the lake of fire, we prevent more people, like those from your ex-community, from becoming Messiahs."

Agrell's guilt gripped her soul like a crushing vice of iron. She choked back the sobs that threatened to send her into another fit of tears, and she said, "I'm so sorry that your people have been victims. I felt such a sense of wonder for the world when I was leaving my home, but in a matter of days, I have been shown how horrible people can be to each other."

She took a deep breath and continued. "I think that's why; I think that answers your question. I've seen people be so horrible that all I want to do is help those in need."

Lahari seemed to consider Agrell's words.

Agrell looked into Lahari's yellow eyes and added, "I don't think you're a monster." ★

Chapter 18 - Massacre

"I can hear the cosmic music from the radiation of the universe." A woman was speaking and her voice echoed from multiple locations along the alley where she was cornered. "I can taste the elements that burn in the stars." She sounded like a goddess. "I see the world; I can see eons. I look into distant corners of alien galaxies." There was wrath in her words, and they reverberated against the old concrete walls.

There was also wrath in her weapons. Black discs of shadow hovered in the air like holes punched in reality, voids in the atmosphere. From them protruded headless skeletal torsos of smoke that were armed with weapons made out of darkness. The woman's Shift powers were horrific.

The apparitions impaled with spears, slashed with swords, and crushed with clubs and maces. Demifae flesh was severed and pierced by the void warriors, and the cries of the dying rang out through the nearby streets of Teshon City. Bodies were broken, limbs were lost, and skulls were smashed by the shadow weapons.

Any survivors of the massacre who tried to drag themselves away from the chaos were nailed to the pavement by massive pikes of smoke. All who entered that alleyway were utterly ruined, butchered by headless enemies against whom they were powerless.

From his position of observation, Talin helplessly watched the evisceration of his underprepared team. The individual they were supposed to be hunting slaughtered them all, and Talin cursed his Demifae enhancement, giving him a perfect view of the devastation that befell his crew.

Claw One was decapitated.

Claw Two's arms were both lopped off above the elbows. She fell to the pavement, writhing and screaming for a moment, but she was skewered and fell still with her blood surrounding her.

Claw Four was smashed and slashed. He turned to flee for the mouth of the alley but was hamstrung, and he crashed to the street.

He roared in agony, but he activated his Demifae regeneration ability and focused it on his grievous injuries.

Horrible weapons of darkness cleaved Claws Five, Six, and Seven, and their bodies fell mangled to the grimy gutter.

Claw Four was trying to crawl away and heal himself, as the woman who was supposed to be the hunters' prey stepped up and stood over him.

"Where are the others?" she asked him in a voice that came from all around.

She did not wait for his reply, as another shadow hole opened, and a headless torso rose from it. A massive battle-axe was gripped in the apparition's bony fingers. It swung the weapon over where its head would have been, and like a guillotine, it brought the blade down on the man's ankles.

Claw Four screamed like a lobster being boiled, as his feet were removed from his legs. He attempted to use his ability of healing, but it was utterly futile against the woman's onslaught.

She asked again. "Where are they?"

"Fuck you!" he spat.

Without hesitation, her monster of darkness made another terrible cut with its axe.

Claw Four shrieked, as both his legs were chopped through the femurs above his knees.

"Who's out there?" she snarled above him.

"Talin!" Claw Four bawled and reached forward.

Dammit, thought Talin.

"Who is that? Where is he?" She repeated herself with a snarl. "Where is he?!"

The shadow torso struck again with its axe, sinking through the meat and bone of Claw Four's shoulder. The slice took off his arm.

He whimpered and pointed up at the rooftop only a few blocks away where Talin was perched.

She looked up and saw the man's shocked face staring back at her, as the battle-axe of shadow fell like an avalanche on Claw Four's neck. His head rolled away.

Talin's enhancement allowed him to see every detail about her, including the expression of righteous malevolence that was scrawled across her face.

In a flash of darkness, another disc appeared in the air beside Talin, and one of her creatures thrust its spear through his heart. His eyes bulged and he gasped, as the headless apparition disappeared, and Talin fell from the rooftop and landed in a crumpled mess on the pavement✪

Chapter 19 - Theolan

Agrell and Lahari were both shuffling through the short tunnel that let out above the waterline, and they were surprised to hear the sound of muffled voices echoing into the mouth of the tunnel.

Agrell turned and asked Lahari, "What is that?"

"Sounds like people talking."

"It sounds like shouting."

They came to the opening and Agrell stepped out onto the stone path below the railing along the walking trail.

A man was standing on either side of Lahari's stepfather, and the two were menacing him. One was holding a pipe, and he jabbed the end against Theolan's chest.

"I don't believe you," the attacker sneered.

"It's true," Theolan pleaded. "I don't have anything. I don't have any money."

The other man was holding a chain, and he whipped it at Theolan.

The metal links slammed against his shoulder and back, and Theolan cried out in pain. He fell to his knees.

"Fuck him up!" the man shouted.

Lahari peeked above the edge of the path, as the assailant swung his pipe overhead.

"No!" she screamed.

Everyone except Agrell was then surprised; the pipe did not move. Her fingers were wrapped around the metal, and her thin arm would not budge, as the man tried to wrench his weapon from her grip.

Then it was Agrell's turn. The man's fingers were like soft dough, as the pipe was ripped from them. Agrell pulled her arm back with such force, that as she released her hold on the makeshift weapon, the pipe flew whistling through the air clear across Widdershins Bay. It slammed against the opposite rock wall with a ringing clang that echoed out over the water.

The man was next. Agrell grabbed his waistband and tugged. In the same manner as the pipe, she hurled him out over the bay, and he fell with a splash into the deep water.

Then the chain hit the side of Agrell's face and wrapped around her neck.

In an instant, she hunched down and launched herself straight at the other attacker. She slammed into the man with such force that he flew back. His body crashed against one of the old walls of stone, and he crumpled to the pavement.

Agrell reached a gentle hand down to Theolan, and he looked up at her like he was staring into the face of a goddess. She carefully helped the bruised and bloody man to his feet, and Agrell held Lahari's battered stepfather close to help him keep his balance.

"This is all my fault," she exclaimed. "I shouldn't have stayed down below talking with your daughter for so long. I was just trying to get to know her, and I left you up here and you were attacked! I should have come up sooner."

"You're one of *them*?" Lahari whispered from where she peered over the edge of the footpath. "You're a fucking Messiah?"

Agrell turned to her, and her eyes filled with tears. "I didn't know," she choked. "A week ago, I didn't know how a Messiah becomes this way. All the mysteries of the community were kept secret until I was in the middle of the ritual. That's when they killed my cousin."

Theolan mumbled at her side, "You're my savior."

"Take him home," Lahari commanded. She stared between Agrell and Theolan, hesitating with an expression that Agrell could not decipher, before Lahari returned to the underground.

"You're... you're my savior," Theolan repeated.

Agrell helped him back to the apothecary.

"Baby!" cried the mystic in dismay, as the front door to his shop opened. "What happened?!" he squawked.

"I left him alone for too long," Agrell declared, and tears poured down her cheeks. She told the others what happened.

"Well, I for one," the mystic replied, "am relieved that you went back up when you did. You rescued Theolan," and he gingerly kissed his injured husband, "from what would have been much worse. Thank you, Agrell. And those men may have been vicious brutes," the mystic added, "but I'm glad you didn't kill *both* of them. At least the one can swim back to shore."

However, Agrell asked, "Swim?"

"Yes, swim, can't you swim?" he asked her.

"No."

"Oh," he replied, "so, you threw him out in the water," the mystic clarified, "yourself not knowing how to swim. Were you expecting that he also did not know how to swim?"

There was a momentary pause while everyone looked at Agrell.

Dozi commented and broke the awkward silence. "I mean, they were just going to do it again to someone else," she said, and she turned to Agrell. "I guess your secret's out now with these two." She jabbed her thumb toward the mystic and his husband.

"Lahari knows too," Agrell added. "I want to go back and talk to her about it."

Dozi sucked air through her teeth. "I don't think that's a good idea."

"I need to explain it to her," Agrell interjected, "and I don't need anyone to come with me," she added in a gentle tone, looking at Theolan and the mystic. "Now I can find my way there and back on my own."

She left the shop, returned to the pipe, and crawled through the tunnel. After climbing out behind the hinged door, Agrell tested the release that Lahari showed her down by the floor. It opened for her, but she closed it again and headed to the top of the stairway.

Lahari was nowhere to be found in either the hall or the stairs below. Agrell called out quietly, but she was met by only silence. Lahari was gone ★

Chapter 20 - Madame Hart & the Principal Messiah, Part One

Behind the massive desk in the leadership chamber, the heads of the hunters were stirred up in a rage. The head woman was standing with her palms on the desk again, leering over it at her kneeling subordinate.

"What do you mean that Talin's entire team is dead?!" she fumed.

"Affirmative, milady," replied the scout with his head bowed.

"How?!"

"They were cut to pieces, literally pieces. There were body parts everywhere, heads, arms…" The man's voice faded.

She glared down at him. "By a single Shift? One Shift managed to accomplish all that carnage?"

"Unclear, milady," the scout continued, "but they all seemed to be attacked by similar weapons, which we could not identify."

The woman looked toward her fellow leadership seated to both sides of her at the table. "I think it's time," she said, and she paused. She looked at the other leaders' faces. "No objections? It's settled. I shall take the title of Madame Hart and reach out to our connection at the Messiah temple."

The woman who was now Madame Hart crossed her arms over her chest. "Too long we have worked from the background," she declared, "acted behind the scenes, but we have been in discussions about grander events," she paused for dramatic effect, "events that will change the world. The time has come, and our combined powers shall be such that none will be able to stand against us. We are going," and her voice took on a wrathful tone, "to war!"

Without another word, Madame Hart stormed around the desk and through the center of the hall. She exited the warehouse and strode with determination the short distance across the industrial district. Teshon City's high tower came into view.

The massive steel doors at the base of the Messiah temple were closed, but Madame Hart was not going to enter through anywhere except the front. The minor door around the side was for the common people. She banged on the metal of the front entrance.

A small window opened and the Tower's porter looked at her through it without a word.

"I am Madame Hart, Master Mystic of Teshon City. I am here to speak with the Principal Messiah."

"What the fuck do you want?" the man snapped.

Madame Hart stood proud before the doors. "The Demifae are going public," she replied.

"More public than an entire neighborhood?" he scoffed. "More public than apothecaries on every corner? By the by," he added, "where's your shop? Oh," he continued, without letting her reply, "that's right, you lot don't even live in the Spritehood with the rest of your Demifae kind. Why is that?" he questioned with a sneer.

"I'll speak no more with you," Madame Hart declared. "Open these doors," she commanded.

The man slammed the little window, and for a moment nothing happened. Then the huge metal doors began to shift. The porter was opening them from the inside, and even though Madame Hart understood the capabilities of Messiahs, she was still amazed to see the scrawny little man moving the massive door with ease. He stepped back, and she touched the metal. She leaned into the open door to see if it would budge. It did not, and the man snickered at her. He did not say another word.

"Greetings and welcome," came the voice of a woman.

Madame Hart looked to a flight of stairs. First appeared a pair of bare feet, then legs in dark trousers, then a torso and the rest of the woman came into view. She was dressed all in fine black leather. The pants were fitted over her muscular legs, and the jacket she wore was snug about her midsection. The zipper was only pulled about halfway up, and the woman's cleavage was exposed. She descended toward Madame Hart and continued speaking.

"I am Wrostecorite, Principal Messiah, and I welcome you to the Messiah Tower. Please, introduce yourself and tell me why you have come to our temple today."

"I am Madame Hart, Master Mystic of Teshon City," she repeated. "We Demifae will no longer tolerate the Shift presence in our city, and we are escalating our vigilance."

"Please," the Principal Messiah said, "join me for tea," and she led Madame Hart into a private chamber. "I thought the leader of the Demifae was the High Chemist," she commented, as the two women took a seat at a table. "Master Mystic is a new term to me. Do you speak for all Demifae?" She turned to an attendant. "We'll take two."

Madame Hart replied, "I speak for the most zealous."

"Ah, zealotry is a quality I admire," the Principal Messiah declared, and her face curled into a wicked smile.

Their teas arrived and each of them took a sip.

Madame Hart furrowed her brow. "What is this? It just tastes like hot water."

"It is," the Principal Messiah replied, "hot water with a single other ingredient." She elucidated in a growl, "One drop of spinal fluid from a living Shift."✪

Chapter 21 - Auntie Peg

Agrell, Dozi, and Ilya made the short trek across the Spritehood to the mystic's shop the following four mornings. On each visit, Ilya received treatment, and Agrell looked for Lahari. Each day, she walked to the waterfront, entered the pipe, and descended the underground stairs to the cave-in where the two young women first met. There was never any sign of Lahari, but Agrell kept insisting to search for her.

Dozi did not readdress her desire to become a Demifae, and neither the mystic nor his husband brought up their discussion from a few days prior. Dozi knew that the two men were right.

Despite having known Ilya only a matter of days, Dozi already felt that a new little family unit was growing with her and the two other young women. She could never kill Ilya; in fact, Dozi knew that she would defend Ilya if she was ever in danger.

She still wished to be more than a mere human, but she knew the mystic was right that the cost to achieve it outweighed the benefits. Ilya's mantis gland was not worth more than the rest of Ilya.

On the fourth day, when Agrell again found no trace of Lahari, she decided to ask the mystic about Auntie Peg. Even though the mystic told Agrell that she did not need to refer to him by his full first name, it had stuck in her mind.

"Tophilogin, your daughter mentioned someone else who escaped the cult." The word was getting more comfortable in Agrell's mind, and she no longer considered *community* to be an appropriate term. Agrell was building a real community around her with Dozi and Ilya, but she also felt close to the mystic and Theolan, and maybe even Lahari.

"Oh, you mean Auntie Peg?" the little round man asked with a beaming grin. "She's a peach of a lady!" he declared. "Brews some of the strongest coffee I've ever enjoyed. And yes, she's one of them," he confirmed, "an ex-cultist. Helped a few others escape as well, if I'm not mistaken."

Agrell's jaw dropped at the information. "There's more of us?"

"My dear," he replied gently, "you didn't think everyone simply bought into the Lovegood ideals, did you? No, no, no, that's the kind of deception that a cult spreads about itself." The mystic put on an eerie voice and dramatically recited, "No one has ever left our midst, because we hold the truth and all who hear it cannot help but believe! Or something like that, right?" he asked Agrell with a chuckle.

She was dumbfounded. "Is Auntie Peg a Shift who escaped?"

The mystic furrowed his brow. "No, she's like you," he replied. "She has told me her story before, but I can't remember the details. She's been away from them for quite a long time. I've heard her say 'more than a decade' on several occasions. She's a wonderful, sweet, and compassionate woman. I think at some point, like you, she realized that they were doing some pretty awful things, and she left. That's my vague memory of her story, anyway."

"Charming lady," Theolan added, "she's so elegant."

The mystic smiled wide. "And what a chef!" he said, smacking his lips and rubbing his round belly. "Auntie Peg has a shop right 'round the corner. I'd be delighted to bring you to see her."

"That would be very kind," Agrell responded, "but would you mind if I ask her some questions in private?"

The mystic took her meaning. "Of course, my dear," he said with a knowing nod. "I can't even begin to imagine what you've gone through, even though you've shared some of it with us. I will certainly leave you two to talk. It will be so good for you to have another person who can relate to some of what you've experienced."

While the mystic patched up Ilya with fresh salves and bandages, Agrell went to the pipe to look for Lahari before visiting Auntie Peg. When she returned, Ilya and Dozi were already prepared to head back to the basement that the three of them now called home.

"Why don't you go visit this other person," Dozi recommended to Agrell. "You can meet up with us later, now that you know your way around the Spritehood."

"Thank you," Agrell replied.

Theolan remained behind at the shop, as Dozi and Ilya headed one direction, and Agrell and the mystic went the other way.

The little round man hooked his hand into the hinge of Agrell's elbow, and she liked feeling the physical connection to him. The two of them were close to the same height, but his stocky thick body was wide, and his whole side was against her. He was jolly and soft and sweet; Agrell thought the man was like a living embodiment of that gorgeous piece of cake he shared with her when they first brought Ilya to his shop.

"It's just this way," he said in a singsong voice, and a moment later, he was pulling open a door and stepping back to allow Agrell to enter.

There was a hand-painted sign in the window.

"Werk! Hey, gurl!" called out a flowery voice.

"Peggy!" the mystic replied in delight. He walked right up, and the two gave each other air kisses on either cheek. Then he stepped back with a dramatic gasp and gave Auntie Peg a once over with his eyes. "Who gave you permission to be so breathtaking?" he asked. She curtsied as the mystic added, "Oh, duchess, and your tuck is so cunt!"

"Thank you, a lady's gotta take good care of her coochie!" Auntie Peg replied with a wink, and she wiggled her fingers at the front of her skirt that billowed up and revealed her panties.

That's a man, Agrell thought to herself.

The mystic stepped back and declared, "Allow me to introduce you to my new young friend, Agrell," and he extended an arm in her direction. "This fine woman is Auntie Peg."

"Charmed!" Auntie Peg proclaimed. Her voice was deep, and even though she was indeed womanly, she was not trying to hide or disguise her voice. She towered over both Agrell and the mystic, never mind that Auntie Peg was also wearing heels on her feet and a tall wig. Her hair was a huge bright pink beehive with curls dangling and bouncing at the sides.

She ran her fingertip along her jawline and fluttered her eyes, showing off her dramatic lilac eye shadow with black cat-eye lines and violet contouring on her cheeks that sparkled with glitter. There was also a shimmering line straight down the length of her nose.

Auntie Peg said about herself, "She's glad she decided to doll herself up and do her makeup this morning. Got her fish face on!" She puckered and blew them a kiss. "A lady's gotta look good when meeting new folks. I can tell that you two are just gagging over how stunning I am!" She winked, turned her head to the side, and brought her fingertip to the end of her nose. "I mean, look at this profile."

"You've never looked more beautiful," the mystic replied to her.

Auntie Peg's skin was coated in a pristine layer of makeup that smoothed her face and made her age difficult to guess. Her lips were vibrant red and she exaggerated their natural shape by applying lipstick slightly beyond their borders. She reached out a large hand to Agrell and took hers with a dainty grip. Auntie Peg smiled.

She was dressed in a voluminous skirt made from purple fabric with large pink polka dots. Beneath it was layer upon layer of tulle in many shades of lavender and periwinkle, and they kept the garment fluffed out from her hips. It was cinched around her waist and a corset squeezed her massive breasts that bulged with excessive cleavage. Agrell could not understand how the person who was clearly a man was also made up of woman parts.

The pair of spiked high heels, which were a shade of soft pink, further accentuated Auntie Peg's impressive height. She was graceful on her feet. Her legs were visible beneath the fabric of her skirt, and they were smooth and muscular. Agrell was confused, and even though her mind told her that Auntie Peg was a man, she thought the woman was beautiful.

"I think you two have quite a bit in common," the mystic commented.

"Oooh," Auntie Peg cooed, "do tell!"

She reached out and Agrell admired the long nails that decorated the ends of her fingers. Each was painted pink and purple to match her dress, with tiny stars or crescent moons or sunbursts, but her thumbnails were both painted with rainbow swirls.

"I'll let you get to know each other a little," the mystic stated.

Auntie Peg looked aghast. "You're leaving?!" she squawked. "I won't hear of it! I've made a lovely pot of stew, and I *insist* you stay and have some with Agrell and me."

The mystic sucked air through his teeth. "Your cooking is so fierce!" he proclaimed. "And as much as it pains me not to eat it with you, I really think you'll have a better conversation without me."

"Bitch, please!" Auntie Peg said to him with a laugh. "This stew ain't gonna eat itself!"

"Agrell," the mystic said, turning to her, "why don't you tell Auntie Peg your last name."

The two made eye contact and the woman looked curious about her.

"Lovegood," Agrell said.

Auntie Peg's expression became less dramatic. "Oh, my dear," she said in a delicate voice, "did you run away?"

The mystic smiled at them and showed himself out of the shop as the women began to talk.

"Come tell me all about it," Auntie Peg requested, "over a bowl of food."

Agrell's stomach was grumbling, and lunch sounded wonderful. "Thank you," she replied.

"Alright," Auntie Peg said, as she placed two bowls of steaming stew onto a table in the back of her shop, "tell me more."

Instead, Agrell asked her own question. "Are you a man?"

"Oh, honey," Auntie Peg responded with a chuckle, "this man is a queen." She smirked, raised her eyebrows, and batted her extended lashes. "Like the boys," she said, waving toward the door that the mystic just exited through, "I'm attracted to men, but as far as my persona is concerned, I'm more in the middle. My feminine side is an important aspect of who I am, and I love showing it off to the world." She flashed a glamorous smile.

"When I get undressed at night," Auntie Peg elucidated, "mama releases her tuck, and she hangs up her fake titties." She gave her very realistic and very large breasts an exaggerated squeeze, and she stuck out her tongue at Agrell. "Then I wash off this sickeningly gorgeous makeup, so in the morning I can beat on a fresh face and look dusted for any customers who pop in to see me." Auntie Peg smiled as if an adoring crowd was admiring her.

"I'm a queen," she repeated with a grin, "but this queen didn't come out of me until much later in life." She held the back of her hand up to the side of her mouth in a dainty expression. "Can you possibly believe," Auntie Peg whispered, "that I'm 40?" She laughed aloud and took a bite of stew. "But tell me about you," she said.

Agrell did not know where to start and opted for another question. "When did you leave the cult?"

"A full 12 years ago," Auntie Peg replied. She was happy to answer Agrell's questions.

"You were there for ten years longer than I was," Agrell commented. "I don't..." she hesitated and looked Auntie Peg up and down. "I don't remember someone like you from when I was a kid," she concluded.

Auntie Peg smirked. "I was living my life fully as a man at that time. I wore the cult clothes and grew my hair long, just like you, but it was never this fabulous!" She ran one hand up the side of her massive beehive wig.

She continued. "It was my responsibility to care for the tweens, but I also don't remember you, must not have gotten you in my group before I was planning to leave. I was raised there, I suppose, just like you?" she questioned and eyed Agrell, who nodded with her mouth full of the delicious rich stew.

"In my own tween years," Auntie Peg went on, "I and another boy in the cult began experimenting together. We were caught kissing, and the leadership paraded us around as the rest of the cult members insulted and ostracized us. They tried to ridicule our desires out of us." Auntie Peg then added in a deflated tone, "He fled, was caught, and killed."

"I'm sorry," Agrell managed thickly through a bite of food.

Auntie Peg took a deep breath before continuing. "I was terrified, and for years I managed to repress my true feelings and my true self, by putting all my focus into the cult. I allowed my own individuality to diminish. I thought that was what was right and good, to deny those urges that the cult deemed abhorrent. For longer than I like to admit, I was a zealous member."

"Are you a Messiah?" Agrell asked cautiously.

"Of course," Auntie Peg replied without hesitation. "Are you?"

Agrell did not respond.

"Look, girlie," Auntie Peg said in a kind voice, "I know how the Lovegoods work. I was a key member for a long time. You don't need to hide from me." She reached out across the table and took Agrell's hand.

Agrell dropped her head and replied, "Yes," she said, "they made me one too."

"I'm so sorry, child. They are horrible people, and you are an inspiration to others for having left!" She looked right into Agrell's eyes. "Do not blame yourself for anything you experienced at their hands. It took me a long time to deal with what the cult put me through. Some days I still struggle with forgiving myself for repressing my true nature for so long. That's part of why I dress like a fabulous queen, to make up for lost time."

"I didn't think anyone ever left before me," Agrell said in a befuddled voice. "I thought I was the only one."

"The way cults and religions and other *isms* keep members," Auntie Peg replied, "is by lying. They all lie outright to their people, but the people don't know any better than to believe the lies." She shook her head. "They literally don't possess the capacity *not* to believe. I'm proud of you for getting away from them!" she declared.

The two of them talked through the afternoon and into the evening. Agrell shared her tragic story, and they both shed tears together. Auntie Peg made them dinner, and it was already dark outside when Agrell finally said goodbye to the glamorous woman. She looked forward to spending more time with her in the near future.

Agrell walked through the quiet streets. Several lamps burned overhead that cast flickering shadows around the alleyways, but the light did little to illuminate her path. However, it was not long before Agrell made it to the entrance of Dozi's basement home, and she slipped inside.

That night, while the three women were asleep in the cold darkness, Lahari appeared★

"Agrell!" Lahari whispered, and the three sleepers awoke.

"What the fuck?" Dozi snapped with a start, and she repeated herself when she came face to face with Lahari's frightening appearance in the shadows. "*What the fuck?!*"

Agrell jumped up, grabbed a candle and Lahari's hand, and she pulled her into Dozi's kitchen area.

Lahari was startled by the physical contact, but she followed.

They could hear Dozi and Ilya whispering harshly to each other but could not make out their words.

"I've been looking for you," Agrell said to Lahari. Their hands separated. "I kept going back to your tunnel, but I couldn't find you! I wanted to let you know that Theolan is okay. Those men hurt him a little bit, but it was not too bad."

Lahari raised her scaly hand. "Agrell," she interrupted, "that's not important right now, and for the time being I've come to terms with you being a Messiah." She looked at Agrell with her sparkling yellow eyes. "We were just attacked in the underground," she declared.

"What? What do you mean?" Agrell asked. "Attacked by who?" She then added, "How can I help?"

"I don't know who they were, but there were a lot of them, and there were definitely Messiahs among them. I saw my people being abducted." She took a breath. "I ran and found the secret crevice in the bedrock near the well that you told me about. I couldn't think of anything else to do except to get out of the underground."

"I'm so glad you did," Agrell replied, and she interlaced her fingers with Lahari's.

Lahari looked down at their hands and asked, "That doesn't bother you?"

Agrell flashed her a puzzled face. "I don't know what you mean," and she restated her offer. "I just want to help however I can."

Dozi stepped up behind them.

"What's going on? You're Lahari?" she asked, but her eyes were fixed on Agrell.

"I am," Lahari replied. "I'm sorry to have barged in here while you were all sleeping, but there was an attack on the underground," she repeated. "I fled."

"We need to help them!" Agrell implored.

"You're outta your mind!" Dozi snapped. "I'm not getting involved in some crazy Shift war! I was willing to open my home and let you use it to visit your family," she said, and Dozi found it difficult to look at Lahari, "but I do not intend to be recruited into a ragtag army. I'm just a human!" she stated.

"But I'm not," Ilya declared, stepping up behind Dozi with the crutch under one arm, "and I'm willing to fight, or help in whatever way I can, also."

"Ugh!" Dozi grunted. She looked at Agrell, then Ilya, and she even tried to look into Lahari's yellow eyes. "*Fine*," she conceded, "I guess I'm in, too. What do we do first?"

"Thank you," Agrell replied, now taking Dozi's hand.

"Alright, alright, skinny girl," Dozi said, pulling her fingers free, "I feel like you *force* me to be a better person than I am," and she rolled her eyes at Agrell. "Please don't get me killed. What do you want to do now?" she asked Lahari.

"I want to go tell my fathers what's happened. They'll be able to help."

"They will?" Ilya asked. "They both seem too gentle for a fight."

"It's less about them, and more about who they are."

"Why, who are your dads?" Dozi asked.

Lahari informed the other three women, "They are leaders of UBHS."

"What's that?" Agrell asked.

"They are a foundation that supports Shifts and works to protect them," Lahari explained.

Ilya scoffed. "Nothing the UBHS ever did has made a difference in my life," she commented.

"Let's take her to her dads," Agrell encouraged, "before the sun comes up."

Lahari wrapped herself in a thin garment that barely hid her uniqueness, and she began to climb up the stairs from Dozi's basement toward the sleeping city above.

"Wait," Agrell called after her, and she grabbed the cloak that she stole on her escape from the cult. "This will work better." She helped Lahari put it on, adjusting the hood and pulling the collar snug.

Lahari was not used to being cared for by anyone, and she looked at Agrell with a peculiar gaze.

Then the four women slipped out into the dark city, and soon they arrived at the mystic's apothecary. Lahari unlocked the door and they all crept upstairs. She knocked on her fathers' bedroom door.

"Ada," she called out in a quiet voice and repeated, "ada."

Rustling sounds from the room were followed by a muffled, "Lahari, is that you, my little moth?"

"Yes, ada."

"Come in! Is something wrong?" he asked as Lahari opened the door and slipped through.

After a few minutes, she reemerged and told the other three women that her fathers were coming out to talk with them.

"It is time to call together the members of Unity Between Humans and Shifts!" the mystic declared, as he and his husband came out in matching silk robes. "This violence cannot be tolerated!"

"Shouldn't we wait until morning?" Dozi asked.

"Certainly not!" replied the mystic. "Those villains did not wait until morning!"

"I agree," Theolan declared. "The city is under attack by a fringe group of its own citizens. We need to do what we can to put a stop to it!"

The women returned to the shop below while the men set about dressing themselves. A few moments later, the mystic and Theolan descended the stairs. Theolan was wearing a bright yellow tailcoat.

"Honey," the mystic said, "the goldfinches and canaries will be jealous of you when they wake up!"

There was still over an hour until the pre-dawn glow before sunrise would begin to lighten the sky.

"Hearing about the attack on the underground has given me such a case of the *morbs!*" Theolan declared. "I couldn't help but dress in something bright." He then turned to the four young women. "We will rally everyone in the UBHS. You'll be able to find us at the

Spritehood meetinghouse, once the birds are awake," he added, giving his husband a little slap.

"We will join you there," Agrell stated. She turned, reached out, and took Lahari's hand again. "Take us to where the attack happened, maybe we can help some of your people."

"No, thank you," interjected Dozi. "I have no interest in getting involved in the middle of a battle between those empowered groups."

Agrell turned to her. "Maybe you should go with them," she recommended, pointing toward the mystic and his husband. "I don't want you to get hurt." Her eyes were full of concern.

Lahari added, "I don't know about this idea, Agrell. You want to help because you're a Messiah, and your strength might actually make you *able* to help, but I wouldn't be surprised if my people do not see what you're offering as assistance, and instead, they attack you."

"I can't just sit here and do nothing!" Agrell proclaimed. "Please, take me somewhere that I can do some good."

"I'm in, too," Ilya declared. "I know I'm not in great shape," she said, with her hand at her bandaged side, "but if I can fly again, I can be your lookout."

"You can fly?!" the mystic asked in surprise.

"We can discuss that later," Agrell stated. "Take me to the fighting."✪

Chapter 23 - Madame Hart & the Principal Messiah, Part Two

"Fall back, warriors!" roared Madame Hart.

"Affirmative!" confirmed the Principal Messiah. "We got more than we came for! Get topside, now!" she shouted.

The small army of enhanced Demifae and Messiahs abandoned their dead. They left the carnage and the darkness, for the fading light of the setting sun above. Several Biological Shifts chased after them and even managed to slay a few more of the invaders before they made it to the surface. The surviving Demifae and Messiahs hauled their prisoners aboveground and through the streets to the Messiah Tower.

"Bring them before us," commanded the Principal Messiah.

"Nine," Madame Hart declared with a wicked smile, as the incapacitated Biological Shifts were dragged into the room. She made a disgusted noise. "Aren't they hideous?" she spat.

Chained and unconscious, each of the nine individuals was unique.

"They're repulsive," the Principal Messiah agreed. "Efficient work and a successful mission," she declared to those gathered.

Their prisoners consisted of a man covered in thick fur like a bear, another with smoke rising from his exposed skin, and a third with four arms. There was also a teenage boy whose epidermis was reflective like liquid mercury. There were also two women prisoners. One of them was animalistic in appearance. Her eyes were massive, but they were closed. Claws grew out of the ends of her fingers, and she also possessed a tail. The other woman was grey-skinned and stony, as if she was carved from marble.

There were three more Biological Shifts, but their physiological changes were even further beyond their kin's. One body seemed to be entirely comprised of overgrown plants. A second sprawled like a pile of dead animals made of wings and eyes and boneless limbs and weird flesh.

Madame Hart pointed at the last prisoner. "That one," she said.

"Where do you suppose its mantis gland is located?" the Principal Messiah questioned.

The two women stood over a motionless machine.

"Dismantle it," ordered the Principal Messiah.

"That's a person," murmured the Biological Shift woman with rock-like skin. She regained consciousness, but the brutal fist of a Messiah plowed into her head and knocked her out again.

"Bring tools!" called Madame Hart.

The unified goal of the Messiah and Demifae attack was not to massacre, but to capture. In the assault, 42 Demifae along with 17 Messiahs brought all-out war to the underground. They left with nine Biological Shift prisoners and left behind 23 Demifae corpses and two dead Messiahs.

While making their initial plans, Madame Hart tried to persuade the Principal Messiah to simply slay as many Biological Shifts as possible to take their heads. In the end, the leader of the

Messiahs convinced her to strive toward the common goal of taking captives alive. The Messiahs wanted living Shifts for experimentation.

The two women led the attack, and secrecy was not their intention. The moment their small army arrived and entered the underground, the Biological Shifts were aware of them, and the unlucky pair on guard duty was brutalized by the oncoming horde. The Messiahs were armed with clubs and bludgeons, and their enhanced strength made their blows devastating. Ranged weaponry would have been worthless in the tight turning tunnels of the Teshon City underground.

The two guards were quickly subdued, but not before they eviscerated one Demifae with eldritch energies, and another was pummeled with a barrage of flying stones. Once they were unconscious, their bodies were dragged over the dead Demifae, and they were pulled from the underground.

As the army penetrated deeper, they found and clashed with the Biological Shifts who dwelt therein, and there was pandemonium. Cosmically powered individuals faced off against those who stole cosmic powers from others.

The Principal Messiah fought with a battle hammer and a massive metal shield. One of the Biological Shifts fired an energy beam that the Principal Messiah dodged before swinging her terrible weapon. It collided and he crumpled. He was dragged bleeding up to the city above. With her hammer and shield, the Principal Messiah raged farther below, and her fellow Messiahs were beside her.

She watched in horror as one of her companions faced off with a Biological Shift woman with a bird-like appearance. Her underling grabbed the bird woman by the wrists, but instead of trying to break free from the man's grip, she leaned toward him. He screamed in unknown agony. Before the Principal Messiah's eyes, his skin began to bubble and hiss, and the flesh of his arms started to melt.

As he tried to pull away from her, the bird woman grabbed his hands and poured her furious energies into him. His wails of suffering grew weaker, as more of his body began to liquefy. Grotesque lesions formed all over the man's skin, and his hair slid from the dissolving flesh on his skull. Then his eyeballs ruptured in their sockets.

Finally, the bird woman released her terrible grip on the melting man, and she launched into an oncoming group of attackers. Compared to the Messiah with his enhanced resistance and durability, whom she just ruined, those next unlucky targets were mere Demifae. The slightest brush of the feathery protrusions from her skin sliced into them like countless razorblades, and the most minor nick sent them sprawling to the floor and convulsing with foam pouring from their mouths. Their wounds hissed and smoldered, and they died in the darkness of the underground.

The Messiahs and Demifae battled against giants and people who looked more like animals than humans. They fought with elemental entities, and beings who possessed godlike abilities. Despite the superior firepower of the Biological Shifts, the army from above was well-prepared and brutal. The assault was brief, and in minutes it was over. They reached the surface and dragged their prisoners through the streets.

In the Messiah Tower, the two leaders of the unified army stood together over the Biological Shift that appeared to be a machine. The Principal Messiah's eyes moved over to Madame Hart.

"Give me one of the sets of tools!" the Demifae woman demanded. "I want to find this mechanical Shift's mantis gland."

Then things got horrible.

The Principal Messiah turned on Madame Hart, and using her enhanced strength, she punched the Demifae woman so hard that her fist penetrated Madame Hart's guts. The Principal Messiah sank her fingers into the woman's organs and ripped them out with the same terrible force of her strike. Gore sprayed across the wall of the chamber, and her fellow Messiahs attacked.

"You think we are just going to let a mantis gland out of our sight?" the Principal Messiah raged at the dying leader of the fringe group of Demifae. She grabbed one of Madame Hart's hunters and threw him against the wall with such force that the impact cracked the stone. He fell twitching to the ground.

"How dare you even approach us as equals?" she continued. "You're theft of powers through arcane incantations and shoddy witchcraft are no match to the empowerments that we as Messiahs gain. Your arts are a waste!"

All around the room, the remaining Demifae were slaughtered by the Messiahs. Arms were ripped off and used as clubs against the bodies from which they were torn. Skulls were bashed against the walls and the floor until brains oozed from the bone shards. Bodies were pummeled and battered, and soon, only Messiahs remained standing around the nine prisoners. The room was full of Demifae corpses.

The Principal Messiah spat a large glob of phlegm onto the dead Master Mystic.

"Thanks for initiating this little skirmish," she said down to the body. "We'll eventually be able to make nine more Messiahs, after we're done with them." She turned and pointed at the prisoners. "Drag this filth to the elevator and take them to the top, and make sure they stay unconscious."

The doors closed.

"The rest of you, get rid of these bodies in the Grey Shallows," the Principal Messiah commanded of the Messiahs who remained below, and she waved a dismissive hand over the Demifae corpses. "Afterwards, meet me in the preparation chamber. We've got some monsters to decapitate."

She turned and headed up a flight of stairs with several other Messiahs, as the rest of the bloody company removed the dead from the entryway. Within the preparation chamber, the Principal Messiah gave her minions orders.

"Wheel a gurney into the middle of the room. Turn on the syphon and the two pumps. Remove the cover from the drip system and set it up." She turned to her primary officer. "Bring my set of tools and two secondary sets to the top of the Tower."

"Yes, milady," the woman replied. She stuck one case under her arm, grabbed the other two by their handles, and headed out to the stairs.

Several of the others slowly assembled a strange device in one corner, while another pushed the wheeled bed into the center of the chamber.

Despite being already covered in blood from the battle, the Principal Messiah donned a heavy leather apron. She put a fresh set of sheets on the gurney and laid the restraints on top of them.

"I'm ready to cut off some heads," she said, as she tied her hair back.

Another Messiah came racing up the stairs from below and bellowed "Milady! Bio-Shifts have entered the base of the Tower!"

The Principal Messiah and her team abandoned their tasks and rushed out of the preparation chamber.

"The prisoners are secure at the top!" she yelled at her fellow Messiahs. "Now, get back down to the entrance and kill those fucking Shifts!" She added with a growl, "I want their mantis glands."

The group of them turned for the stairs that led below, as devastating bolts of blue energy were unleashed upon them from above ★

Chapter 24 - Rescue

Lahari led Agrell and Ilya from the apothecary through the dark streets of the Spritehood, and to one of the few ways into the underground. The sun was starting to rise over the harbor as they reach the entrance, but they were stopped by a group of Biological Shift guards right inside. Each was unique.

"No one is permitted below," declared an individual with transparent skin and organs; even the bones beneath their flesh were visible.

"It's me," Lahari stated, and she pulled back the cloak that hid her uniqueness.

"We are here to help," added Agrell.

"I can't let you in," the guard replied, "and I'm definitely not allowing humans down here, especially not an injured one." He eyed the crutch under Ilya's arm.

"Looks can be deceiving," Ilya told him.

Lahari stepped up to the guards and stated in a calm voice, "Not only can you *not* stop me from entering," and they all braced themselves against her, "but as far as I can tell, the underground needs as much help as it can get right now."

Agrell and Ilya looked on without understanding the exchange between Lahari and her fellow Biological Shifts.

"Now, move," she commanded.

Then the guard's demeanor changed and he spoke in a pleading voice that was unexpected by either Agrell or Ilya.

"We're under strict orders. There are many dead bodies that we are trying to deal with, and instabilities have occurred in some of the structures below. It's really not safe and..."

"How many of us were killed? Tell me," Lahari demanded.

"Last we heard, there were 14 of our folk unaccounted for, but there was a collapse," the guard added, "some people may be trapped."

"Let us help!" begged Agrell. "I can help, I really can," she reiterated, and she picked up a massive chunk of broken wall in one hand.

This caused all of the guards to activate their cosmic abilities.

"She's a fucking Messiah?!" one of them yelled. His eyes went white and smoke started issuing from them.

"How dare you bring her here?!" screamed another, whose body started to enlarge right before their eyes.

A third guard lashed out with his energies, and a radiance like that of the sun appeared at the entrance to the underground.

Both Agrell and Ilya flinched and cringed away from the luminous assault, but then the light vanished and the guard fell to his knees.

Lahari was standing in front of the other two women with her arms outstretched. She was frowning. The black quills that protruded from her arms and legs and face extended like hundreds of tiny onyx daggers. They moved and flexed threateningly. The young woman's physiological uniqueness even seemed to quell the determination of the guards, and they cowered.

Another one of the men fell before Lahari, but she spoke over whatever protest or pleading they intended.

"We are going into the underground, and you are going before us to announce our arrival." She pulled the guard to his feet. "Now, move," she repeated.

With Agrell and Ilya, she entered the mouth of the underground, and they began to descend. Soon they arrived at the place where the attackers first clashed with the Biological Shifts who live beneath the city. Dried blood streaked the floor, and strange burn marks that were not made by fire scorched the walls and stone steps. There were no bodies.

They headed deeper underground and came to the first congregation of people. The three women could hear the murmur of talking and see the glow of light coming from a chamber ahead, and as they approached they were announced.

The guard stepped into the doorway and declared, "Lahari has come from the city above to help us with a human and a Messiah," but before anyone could respond, Lahari grabbed him by the back of his neck and thrust him up against one side of the doorframe.

"She is not a Messiah," Larahi snarled through gritted teeth, and with her sparkling yellow eyes, she looked over at Agrell. She leaned in very close to the guard's ear and said in a voice loud enough for everyone present to hear, "You will not call her that again." She stepped past him into the room. "Agrell is very strong," Lahari declared, "and she's here to help."

The guard was looking rather shell-shocked, and Ilya stepped up beside him. "I'm not a human," she stated in a proud voice. "I'm a Shift," and she felt uplifted to state that fact aloud. Ilya could not remember having ever said those words before.

Lahari's fellow Biological Shifts informed her that everything was worse farther below, and they continued deeper.

"What happened?" Ilya asked Lahari.

"You mean above?"

"Yeah, what happened with that flash?"

Agrell added, "And why did they all seem afraid of you?"

"I can't exactly explain my power," Lahari replied, "but when I was young, one of the much older Bio-Shifts who I looked up to, said it was like there was a black hole within me. I can absorb energy, including the energies projected by other Shifts, Biological or otherwise. One of those guards up there tried to blast our new friend here," and Lahari nodded toward Agrell, "but I didn't let that happen."

The two made eye contact. "And the reason why they all seem afraid of me," she elucidated, "is because what I did up there was merely a passive display of my energy absorption."

Lahari continued. "There was a man last year who wanted to be with me. We both possessed similar appearances with our skin. However, I knew his reputation, and I wasn't interested in him. At first, that was enough, but he was persistent, and I gave in to him."

Lahari signed before she admitted, "We ended up spending some time together. He wanted more from me than I was ever willing to give, and eventually, he decided to try and take what he wanted by force. Everyone in the underground knew that he had abused a few women in his past, but he swore to me that he had changed, and he would never do anything like that to me. I was young," Lahari added. "I'm still young," she declared, "but he was quite a bit older than me, and stronger than me, and his determination to have me, pushed him to attack me."

Before she could finish her story, they arrived at a large chamber. Many of the underground dwellers were gathered, and they were engaged in a heated discussion, but the guard stepped into the doorway and again announced the three women. Only some of the people present paid any attention to him.

"Lahari has just arrived from the city above with two," he hesitated "others, and they want to help."

One of the leaders stepped up and replied, "We lost people. They took prisoners. If you want to help, you can be part of the rescue mission."

"When is it leaving?" Lahari asked.

"Now," declared one of her fellow Biological Shifts.

Agrell thought the person bore an uncanny resemblance to an elephant. He was large, with skin that was grey and deeply wrinkled. A pair of pale protrusions extended down along both sides of his head that were akin to tusks. The elephantine character stomped towards the stairs.

"They want to treat us like monsters?" he asked them all. "We'll give them monsters!" and he led the group of Biological Shifts with Agrell and Ilya back up toward the city above.

Lahari continued her story with Agrell and Ilya. "He was bigger than me, stronger. Even with my constant denials, he eventually told me that he thought we'd spent enough time together that I owed it to him. He actually told me that I *owed* him my body," she scoffed.

"When I adamantly refused, he forced himself on me. He punched me in the stomach and shoved me down. I couldn't catch my breath, but in order to defend myself, I reached as deeply into my powers as I could."

Ilya stumbled with her crutch and winced at the lingering pain that throbbed from her side. Agrell helped steady her, and Lahari continued.

"Even though he was not using his Shift abilities at the time, somehow I absorbed his energies from within him. He was climbing on top of me when my powers unleashed. He screamed, but once I released my fury, I did not stop syphoning from him until he fell away from me and collapsed."

"Did you kill him?" Ilya asked. "Is that why they're all afraid of you?"

"No, he did not die," Lahari replied. "We now keep him in a chamber."

Ilya looked relieved. "Oh, good, he's locked up."

"Not exactly. The leadership discussed my powers with me after the incident, but we couldn't come up with a clear idea of what happened to him. He's not in a jail cell, but he's also not a threat to anyone anymore. I absorbed his powers, and I continued to draw from him until I no longer felt in danger."

Lahari sucked air through her teeth and said, "You know how I mentioned that he looked like me? His skin was covered with thick stony scales similar to mine, but when I released him from the grip of my powers, he was nothing but a soft pink thing, like a giant embryo. His fingernails and toenails dropped out, and his eyes became useless glassy orbs. He's little more than a vegetable now."

"It sounds like you did something to his mantis gland," Ilya pondered.

"Yes, that's what a few of the leadership suspected happened. I would have killed him," Lahari added in a conclusive but not cold voice. "He deserved to die, but I think his current punishment is appropriate."

"There's more punishment?" Agrell asked her.

"No," Lahari replied, "I just mean that I would have killed him for trying to rape me, and for every other woman who was abused by him before me, but I think it's appropriate that he live out the remainder of his days as a useless giant fetus."

The group emerged from the underground and were greeted by the light of the morning sun that was starting to wake up the city.

"The Tower is this way," someone said, and a few minutes later, they arrived at its base.

A pair of energy beams from two of the Biological Shifts blasted the heavy metal gates open.

Ilya grabbed Agrell and Lahari's hands. "Wait," she said to them, and she pulled the two women back as the rescue party raced inside and found the chamber empty.

She pointed up to the very top of the Tower, and the columned, open-air pavilion that used to be the old base's watchtower. "Look, something's happening up there," she stated. "Let me see if I'm healed enough to use my powers. I'll fly up over there," and she turned and pointed toward one of the tall buildings a little way away, "and see what I can see."

"If you think you're up for it," Agrell said with concern in her voice.

Ilya nodded, and she began to lift off the ground like it was the most normal thing in the world.

Agrell looked on in amazement, as the crutch Ilya was using fell to the concrete, and she rose above their heads.

Lahari's yellow eyes were also sparkling with wonder.

Less than a minute later, Ilya was back with her feet on the earth.

"They're up there!" she declared. "There are a bunch of Bio-Shifts all chained up together at the top of the tower. I could only see one guard, but there must be others."

"I bet I could break the chains," Agrell told them, "if you could fly me up there." Then she realized that Ilya was standing without her crutch. "Hey, look at you!"

"I know," Ilya replied. "I feel better, somehow, but I'm not sure I can carry you up there. And what about the guard?" she added. "However many there are, they are going to be Messiahs. Since you're essentially invincible and as strong as them, I think you will end up in a stalemate at best."

"What if you bring me to the top, and then as you fly off, you drag the guard over the side and drop him to the street." Agrell's timid voice spoke the harsh words, and they were like the threat of rolling thunder from an oncoming storm.

Lahari and Ilya looked up the many stories to the peak of the Tower. "I suppose we could try that," Ilya agreed, but she sounded uncertain.

"I don't think the Messiah will die if you drop him off," Lahari added, "but at least he won't be up there anymore. I'll stay hidden in that alley," and she pointed to a narrow side street. "Come back down and get me after."

Ilya and Agrell wrapped their arms around each other.

"Let's see what happens."

She activated her powers. The two of them lifted into the air and hovered for a moment. Then Ilya soared straight for the top of the Tower with Agrell.

Without letting her feet touch down, she dropped Agrell beside the group of prisoners, and Ilya grabbed the guard. She pulled him, but the man snatched her with strength she could not match, and he threw Ilya over the side. He thought that would take care of one of the surprise attackers, but Ilya flew. She headed down and grabbed Lahari.

"That guard was way too strong for me, but we've gotta get back up there and help Agrell!"

"Let's go!" Lahari cried out, as they sped through the air.

The guard had already overpowered Agrell and was holding her in a headlock. She was on her knees but still conscious. He was a trained soldier, and she was no match for him.

Another Messiah climbed up the stairs and grabbed the unconscious Biological Shift who possessed four arms. Just as Ilya and Lahari landed, the guard stuck his blade into the man's neck.

"No!" screamed Lahari, but the Messiah began to slice, and blood poured onto the floor.

Lahari pulled herself from Ilya's hands, ran at the guards, and she grabbed each of them by their shoulders. She closed her yellow eyes and tapped into the cosmic energies within her.

Her powers consumed.

The two guards shrieked, and Agrell broke free from the one who held her. The men fell to the floor and convulsed in Lahari's grip. She knelt over them, devouring anything and everything that made up their lives. Their voices faded, but still, Lahari held onto the guards.

Before Agrell and Ilya's eyes, the two men's bodies began to deteriorate. Their mass was shrinking, and when Lahari finally released them, she rose and stood above what looked like mummified corpses. However, both of them were still breathing.

Lahari made a sound of contemplation. "My powers seem to be even harsher against Messiahs than they are against my own kind."

The two men wheezed like living skeletons.

Agrell was breaking chains and pulling apart shackles with her bare hands, and Lahari started saying her fellow Biological Shifts' names. She gently slapped their cheeks to help rouse them.

Footsteps from the stairs warned that other guards were almost upon them.

"Use something as a weapon!" Ilya commanded Agrell. "You're strong, but you need an advantage over those other Messiahs."

Agrell looked down at the chain in her hands, and then at the murdered four-armed Biological Shift at her feet. The body was almost decapitated, and the handle of the knife still protruded from the flesh. Blood was pooling around the corpse.

They are killing Lahari's people, Agrell thought.

She screamed and flailed the chain like a whip. It wrapped around the first Messiah's neck as his head came up through the stairwell, and Agrell pulled with all her might.

The guard's neck was unaffected by Agrell's initial assault with the chain, but her subsequent pull yanked him off his feet and through the air. Cannibalizing a Shift's photonova gland grants the eater with nigh invulnerability, but it does not affect the individual's weight.

Agrell released her grip, and the chain and the Messiah sailed out of the tower. This again left her unarmed.

"I need another weapon!"

"Anything can be a weapon!" Lahari barked at her, while still helping her people out of the remaining chains.

Agrell looked at one of the stone columns that supported the upper pavilion's roof. She placed her hands on either side of it, and with her skinny arms, she snapped the massive pillar like it was no more than a twig. Agrell held it like a battering ram and ran to the top of the stairs.

The next Messiah to emerge caught the brunt of her impact in the chest. He was knocked off balance, and Agrell used it to push him over the side of the tower as well. Then she changed her grip on the column and held the enormous thing like a club. She roared in fury and swung it overhead. The stone pillar crashed onto the skull of the next guard. It did little except to slow the Messiah down, but Agrell's attack did enough. She no longer fought alone.

Lahari grabbed the guard by his head, and she screamed, as she ripped his stolen energies from him. His body went rigid in her hands, and his flesh withered like dry leaves in autumn. The man's skin clung to his bones and pulled taught across his face. Lahari continued to draw the lifeforce from him, and his lips peeled away from his teeth. His eyes rolled back and sank deep into his skull. When she released the guard, his body fell back, clattering down the stone stairs.

Agrell managed to free the remaining Biological Shifts. A few of them were in a bad state, but they were all conscious.

The huge man with thick fur stepped to the top of the stairs, and he unleashed multiple devastating bolts of blue energy on the Messiahs below✪

Chapter 25 - UBHS

As the sun was beginning to set, Dozi followed the mystic and his husband into the meeting hall where the Unity Between Humans and Shifts members were gathered. The tension in the air was palpable, and Dozi overheard a few angry remarks.

"The Messiahs' violence needs to be stopped," one man said.

"We outnumber them," added a woman.

"Someone should retaliate," another person suggested.

Several comments of agreement came after a different woman declared, "Messiahs are cannibals."

The head of the organization stepped onto a riser at the front of the room, and she addressed the members. "Good evening, friends," she called out over the murmur of conversation. "Thank you all for coming to this emergency UBHS meeting on such short notice."

All other talking ceased.

"In case any of you have not yet heard," she continued, "a group of Messiahs and Demifae attacked the inhabitants of the underground last night. This villainous action cannot be allowed to go without a response! Their hatred must be countered."

She began to pace across the low stage. "For too long they have lived comfortably, murdering our Shift cousins. Will we continue to stand aside and do nothing? Do we intend to watch more of this great city's citizens slain to grant power to others? And what of that power? The stolen strengths that create Messiahs come from our friends and family."

A few people called out affirmations as their leader continued.

"I may be a human, but I married a Shift, and I know there are many of you in beautiful mixed relationships. We are proof that all peoples can live in peace and harmony. We are the shining example to all others."

Another leader, a tall bearded man, stepped onto the stage beside her and spoke.

"We need to gather as many like-minded people as we can, and we will march in protest on the Messiah Tower. We will meet *not* tomorrow, but the following morning at sunrise, on the Spritehood southern waterfront. Spend tomorrow spreading the word about the march so we can increase our numbers."

The first leader continued. "We will walk the perimeter of the peninsula to the northern side before heading south to the Messiah temple. As always, make signs or banners, dress up however you would like, and remember that if you don't want your identity to be known, it is always appropriate to wear a mask. This is not an act of war, please don't attend armed. We want to inform the city what happened, not cause another confrontation."

Dozi stood off to one side, watching the gathered people, who were all watching the two leaders. Around the room, there were Shifts who were unapologetic and open about their powers, and humans were standing side by side with them. She had never seen such diversity.

In the back of her mind, Dozi still felt that urge and desire to be more than she was. The lecture she received from the mystic and his husband was still fresh in her mind, and now that she befriended her first Shift, someone killing Ilya for the photonova gland inside her head was unthinkable. Dozi also could not deny the horrors of what Agrell went through before escaping the Lovegood cult. Conflicting thoughts swirled in her mind, as the speakers finished and the group began to disperse.

"Will you join us?" the mystic asked, as he and his husband approached Dozi. "Will you be there to march?"

"I don't know," she replied. "I need to find out what happened to Ilya and Agrell."

"As a fellow human," Theolan commented with a little bow, "please allow me to encourage you to not spend too much of your worry concerned with those who are powerful, as they can usually take care of themselves. Please join us," he urged.

She responded with only, "Maybe."

Night began to swallow the city in darkness, and Dozi headed back to her home. It was quite a while since the last time she was there alone, and she could not help but worry about her new friends.

After eating, she crawled into bed and tried to find sleep, but the people she recently met now flashed into her mind. They were starting to feel like *family*.

That was one of the things Dozi greatly desired when she moved away from her home in the mountains, to find a group of people who made her feel complete; this ragamuffin crew of mismatched individuals seemed to encompass that. She never could have imagined that the people she would be close to, would include a Shift and an ex-Messiah. Over the past several days, the mystic and his husband had also firmly lodged themselves in Dozi's heart. Even their Biological Shift daughter drifted through her mind. Lahari's appearance may have been shocking, but she was also fascinating.

In the cold darkness, Dozi dozed off to sleep ★

Chapter 26 - Underground, Part Three

Lahari, Agrell, and Ilya helped the group of freed prisoners limp down the stairs within the Messiah Tower. The other Biological Shifts who were part of the rescue party had dealt with the Messiahs below, and they escorted their kin out the entrance and into the Teshon City streets.

Quite a few people were startled by the sight of them. To most of the abovelanders who were oblivious of the vast community that lived beneath their feet, the Biological Shifts looked like monsters. Many citizens of the city knew nothing about their underground neighbors, and coming face to face with them was shocking. Some people screamed, others jeered and yelled hateful slurs, while still others simply fled in fear.

Eventually, the bloody and bruised group arrived at the mouth of the tunnel that led below, and the guards raced out to help their fellow inhabitants back into the underground.

"Everyone, get inside, quickly!" called out a man with skin that was striped like a tiger.

Agrell supported escaped prisoners on both sides of her. She held them close and helped them get down the stairs into the darkness. They seemed shocked that such a normal-looking girl so readily made physical contact with them, but they did not complain about the assistance.

Soon the group reached the first main chamber, and they all entered. A number of other Biological Shifts came rushing in with bandages, ointments, and potions for the injured. Broken bones were set, and a few gashes received stitches.

Several of the inhabitants were very surprised to see the two abovelanders.

The unique Biological Shift with the appearance of a plant lost consciousness again and slumped to the floor.

One of the men who was giving medical attention to the injured called out, "Someone, give me a hand getting him up onto the table."

"I can do it!" skinny little Agrell offered.

"I need someone probably a little stronger than… *you're a Messiah?!*" he screamed, as Agrell scooped up what looked like a massive tree trunk as if it were light as a feather.

Lahari launched herself in front of Agrell and positioned herself between her and everyone else.

"*No, she's fucking not!*" Lahari roared. She then enunciated very clearly for all gathered to hear, "Agrell is not a Messiah. She is one of us," she said definitively. "Even though she doesn't look like it," and Lahari turned her gaze around the room to each of her fellow Biological Shifts. "She is one of us, and she is *not* a fucking Messiah."

"Keep her away from me," someone said under their breath.

"She's not one of us," another argued in a whisper.

Lahari's black spines flexed and extended.

"I'm just here to help," Agrell pleaded.

Lahari told Agrell, "You keep right on helping."

There was more quiet grumbling from some of the others, but they focused on caring for the injured until they were patched up and bandaged.

"Let's get farther below," one of them urged, and everyone began heading deeper into the underground.

Many now viewed Agrell as a cannibal, and they shot her disgusted or fearful looks. She heard things mumbled under their breath that she knew were about her. More than once, she dropped her head in shame about where she was from, but she tried to focus on the people she was helping.

In the next massive underground chamber, one of the Biological Shifts told everyone that there was a ceremony for the dead, and they should make their way to the well of fire. The group eventually arrived, and the ceremony was already in progress. Bodies were wrapped in white sheets, and an old woman whose skin was covered in thick hair was speaking over the corpses. Giant curling horns grew from the sides of her head.

"We send our friends, families, and loves to the fire."

The giantess dropped one corpse and then another into the well. She lifted the next body from the floor, and enormous tears began to stream down her cheeks.

From the well's opening, a continuous stream of smoke rose and disappeared up the chimney. Then a strange noise began to issue from above everyone's heads. The sound quickly grew into a shrill metallic scream, and they all looked up. Then something shot down from the opening in the ceiling✪

Chapter 27 - New Principal Messiah

Within the tower, the Principal Messiah wailed in bloody agony. She was one of the few still alive.

From around the city, most of the other Messiahs were arriving, those who were not part of her assault on the underground. Only a single Biological Shift was among the dead. The corpse of the man with four arms still lay in a pool of blood at the top of the Tower.

Because Messiahs are virtually invincible, it was not necessary for the Tower to contain any medical facilities. Besides the

Principal Messiah, there were only two others who survived the rescue assault by the Biological Shifts. They lay on separate tables.

One man was silent. His spirit was tipping the balance and beginning to drift away from him. Part of his head was missing. The flesh and bone and brains were cauterized and smoldering. He twitched gently as he approached death.

The other Messiah moaned through gritted teeth, too weak to scream. Both of his arms were gone, and the bandages over his gristly shoulders were seeping with blood, as it slowly drained from him.

The Principal Messiah screamed her suffering to the world. She was sprawled on her stomach with her head turned to one side. Her back was completely flayed of its flesh, and within her exposed ribcage, her lungs ballooned as they wheezed her screams. Her left leg was gone, and the stump was smoking. She was missing one hand, and also an eye, and the hair on the side of her head was scorched away. There was a brutal gash in her side, and its bandage was saturated and dripping blood.

"Release the cataclysm device," she hissed between ragged breaths. "That is my final order as Principal Messiah," but her second in command leaned down near to her.

"We will not," she whispered in her superior's ear. "It will not be *you* who gets that honor; it shall be mine. You will die as the disappointment of Messiahs, the one who got herself and her entire company killed on the schemes of a renegade group of Demifae. No, *Principal Messiah*," and the woman spat the title with disdain, "you are through giving orders."

When the High Chemist of Teshon City arrived, of the remaining three who needed medical attention, only the Principal Messiah was still alive. As the High Chemist entered, she stopped in her tracks, overwhelmed by the shock of what she witnessed. She was the city's most skilled Demifae healer, but rarely did she attempt to treat anything as gruesome.

The High Chemist leaned over the Principal Messiah's open back. The woman was barely bleeding, despite the hideous wound. The bones of her spine and their encased cord were writhing like a dying snake. Her ribs squeezed into her lungs, and with each breath, she screamed. The scorched pink fleshy balloons pushed and bulged into the spaces between the cages of white bone.

"She is not long for this world," the High Chemist said in a low voice.

"Make her passing more peaceful," one of the other Messiahs urged.

"And make it quick," added another.

"As you wish." The woman pulled out a tiny blade and stabbed twice.

The Principal Messiah's eyes bulged and her mouth gaped like a fish, as she gasped at the air that would not remain within her lungs. They slowly deflated.

"*What did you just do?!*" a Messiah shouted and grabbed the High Chemist's wrist.

She cried out in pain, as the empowered fingers broke the bones in her forearm. The short knife clattered to the floor, as she dropped to her knees and declared through her pain, "I did what you asked! She was already going to die, and now her suffering will soon be over."

"How did you even pierce her?" another Messiah asked.

The High Chemist groaned, gripping her mangled arm. "It's a diamond-dagger." She winced and cried out in pain. "I need to get this fixed," she hissed through her teeth.

On the table, the Principal Messiah clawed at the wood with her remaining hand, as asphyxiation slowly dragged her spirit from her ruined flesh. Her body convulsed, and she tried to take a final breath. Then her eyes became unfocused, and she fell still.

The High Chemist left the tower and rushed back out into the city to other healers, as the new Principal Messiah was appointed.

"I solemnly swear to uphold and support the continuation of the Messiah line. I swear to always lead for the good of all Messiahs, above and beyond all other life. I recognize that my responsibility is to my fellow Messiahs, and every other being is below us. I will take on this duty with the most serious mind and conscience."

The new Principal Messiah completed repeating the vows of office, then with a wicked grin, she said, "Release the cataclysm device." ★

Chapter 28 - Death Drop

Deep in the underground, above the well of fire, the object that came spiraling out of the chimney looked like a winged sphere. Gravity pulled it toward the opening that led to the bubbling magma below, and as the thing spun downwards, it produced a shrill whistle.

The noise interrupted the memorial that the Biological Shifts were holding at the well, and no one in the chamber knew what the thing was. The spinning orb traveled from the opening in the chimney to the well of fire in a split second.

The giantess was closest, and she was the first to look over down after it. She watched the thing land and sink into the molten stone.

Then the cataclysm device detonated.

A reverberation shook through the underground chamber. Everyone froze.

"The magma is rising," the giantess growled.

"How can that be?" asked the woman with a bird-like appearance. "Are you sure?" She rushed beside the giantess, looked down, and there could be no doubt.

The fire from below was coming.

"*Everyone, out!*" the bird woman commanded. "Head through the passage and take the stairs up to the meeting chamber. Once there, we can split up and call for a general evacuation of the underground. Now, move!"

Leaving the corpses undisposed, everyone raced to the door. Several of the inhabitants looked back over their shoulders, and Agrell saw their expressions of shock and terror. She turned, just as the stones of the well collapsed and fell through the hole. Magma began to bubble up like a tiny volcano.

"Run!" someone screamed. "It's coming!"

Agrell double-checked to make sure everyone was out of the room, but as soon as the last person stepped into the hallway in front of her, she froze. She looked to Lahari and Ilya and the group of fleeing Biological Shifts, and Agrell's mind raced. She turned back and knew they could not escape the rising magma.

Agrell cared about the inhabitants of the underground, and although the feelings were new to her, she *loved* the people who were now her friends. Ilya and Lahari held special places in her heart. She also came to cherish the mystic and his husband, Theolan, during her few days of freedom.

Then Dozi flashed into her mind. Dozi felt like the other half of Agrell, a sister that she never had, or a lover who only ever required companionship. She wanted to thank Dozi, wanted to tell Dozi how much she helped her to feel free. Agrell wanted to tell Dozi that she was perfect.

The immediate situation forced Agrell into the present. She needed to protect the people who were in imminent danger. She knew they were not going to make it; they were not going to escape the oncoming fire.

For the briefest moment, Agrell thought the Messiahs had won, and that everyone in the underground was going to die.

Then in a flash, she knew this was the moment that would make up for her cousin's murder.

With all her might, Agrell kicked through the stone wall on one side of the doorway, and then the other. Those fleeing turned back to look at what caused the sounds, and they saw the stone shattering.

Agrell reached up, grabbed the lintel, and pulled the entire wall from above her head down into the room with the well. The massive slab slammed down against the floor of the chamber, and she pushed it against the oncoming onslaught of magma.

Everyone stopped to watch the skinny girl, who alone, was trying to hold back one of the most terrible forces in all of nature.

Agrell looked in their direction and screamed, *"Run!"*

Both Lahari and Ilia cried out Agrell's name, and the Biological Shifts who moments ago despised her existence, now realized how wrong they were about her.

"Run!" she screamed again. "Go, go now!"

Hands grabbed Ilya and Lahari, and they were dragged to the stairs that lead up and away from the approaching fiery death.

"Ruuun!!"

Agrell's voice could still be heard as the others made it up the stairs to the meeting chamber.

"Ruuuun!"✪

Agrell turned to the wall and smashed out another enormous section of stone to pile on top of the first. She knew the effort was futile, but she was determined to provide the others with as much time to escape as she possibly could. Multiple slabs of bedrock were ripped from the walls of the chamber by her empowered hands, and each impeded the progress of the magma, as it slowly melted them.

Agrell stepped out into the hall and saw that everyone else was out of sight, but then her makeshift blockade crumbled. She looked all around her, and could see up the short flight of stairs to the cave-in by the narrow crack that now led to Dozi's home.

The magma was going to rise up and penetrate the gap. It was going to destroy the place where Agrell now knew she belonged, and if Dozi was in her basement, it was going to kill her, too.

Agrell leapt up against the stones of the cave-in, again clinging to them like a bat, but this time she pulled. A gargantuan piece of bedrock dislodged, and she brought the thing crashing down in the path of the oncoming river of molten rock. She gripped the stone and screamed down the hall toward the others again, "Run!"

The massive boulder served its purpose and held back the flow. Agrell dug her heels in and pushed against it.

However, the stone did not have time to melt before the raging heat began to cause it to crack. She held the pieces together for as long as possible, with the radiant energy starting to scorch even her virtually invulnerable body.

Agrell growled wordless syllables through her gritted teeth and kept the crumbling pieces together with her bare hands.

The remaining chunks of the boulder that she still held ruptured from the heat, and Agrell closed her eyes.

She thought to herself, *I saved them.*

The wave of magma engulfed and consumed Agrell, as the compromised walls all around gave way. The ceiling collapsed and buried the terrible fire in a mountain of smothering stone ★

Chapter 30 - Misery

Lahari could not remember the last time tears streamed from her yellow eyes, but they now poured down her cheeks. She and Ilya ran with the others up the stairs, and as they arrived in the meeting chamber, they heard a terrible rumbling from down below. Ilya collapsed to a chair and sobbed into her hands, as the bird woman started giving orders.

"You three," she said, pointing at several people, "head down to the netherswamp. You two, go to the werefolk. A few of you need to check purgatory, even though it's not in a good state; there were people working in there. Get everyone to the uppermost chambers of the underground, and get them there quick," she demanded.

Lahari fell to her knees in front of Ilya, leaned her head down, and wrapped her arms around Ilya's waist. As they cried together, Ilya gently stroked Lahari's back where no spines protruded from her skin, and the two shared a moment of sorrow.

"Everyone else, get upstairs *now!*" the bird woman shouted. She pointed to another hallway, and the remaining Biological Shifts headed in its direction.

Lahari rose to her feet, and Ilya took her hands. The two gave each other sympathetic expressions, and even through Lahari's unusual appearance, Ilya could see that she was also heartbroken.

The people who were not sent to alert others of the evacuation made their way along a narrow passage to another flight of stairs. Before long, most of the inhabitants of the underground were in upper rooms close to the surface.

There, they waited.

After a few uneventful hours, several people decided to venture below. They needed to know if the rising magma was still a threat, and they also wanted to assess the devastation to the underground.

"I need to go tell Dozi," Ilya said to Lahari.

"And I want to see my fathers," Lahari added. "Come with me."

She wrapped herself in the cloak Agrell gave her, and a fresh sob wracked her body. She choked it back, but saw that tears were again streaming down Ilya's face.

"I'm sorry she's gone," Lahari whispered.

Ilya let out an inadvertent wail. "Agrell was always the best of us," she said. "Some people struggled to see beyond her past, and you're not the only one," Ilya added with an apologetic shrug. "She died to save us," she whispered.

Lahari reached out and took Ilya's hand. "Agrell sacrificed herself so that we all might survive."

Ilya nodded.

The two women made their way to a secret exit that let them into the basement of an old Oselian military structure. Pipes above their head were rusted, and there was a layer of dust on the empty shelves. Whatever used to be stored in the room was either used up or stolen long ago.

The two young women arrived at street level, opened a back door to the building that led to a dark alley, and Lahari and Ilya slipped out into the Teshon City streets. The sun was just starting to rise.

They were on the opposite side of the Spritehood from where Lahari's fathers lived, but the city was still asleep, and they quickly made their way through the quiet neighborhood. It was not long before they reached and entered the apothecary.

Ilya and Lahari went through a tearful exchange with the two men, as they talked about what Agrell did for them.

The mystic requested of Ilya, "Please bring Dozi back here. We will hold a celebration of remembrance."

Ilya said she would, and she left Lahari in the care of her saddened fathers.

She walked back out under the rising sun. A fishmonger was setting up his cart, and one of the local coffeehouses unshuttered its windows. The barista waved at Ilya. There was a pair of children selling flowers from a basket to the early-morning folk. The city was starting to wake up, and fresh tears burned Ilya's eyes.

No one knew what happened that night; no one knew. No one knew that Agrell was gone. People were all going about their routines and tedious lives, and Agrell was just gone.

Ilya's sobs drew several awkward glances. A few minutes later, she slipped behind the old fan cage and through the hidden entrance to the basement that she had begun to think of as home.

Dozi awoke at Ilya's return. She stretched and yawned when she saw who it was.

"Where's Agrell?"

Ilya sat on the end of her bed. Her tears flickered in the candlelight.

"What's wrong?" Dozi asked. She sat bolt upright. "What happened?"

"I need to tell you something," Ilya began, and her voice was full of grief.

"What?! Tell me!"

"It's Agrell," Ilya said, and her voice broke. She was overcome by woe.

"Oh, no," Dozi whispered.

Ilya took a quavering breath, and between her sobs, she cried out, "She's dead!" Her face fell to her hands and she wailed.

Dozi tentatively brought her hand to Ilya's back and said, "That can't be." Tears welled in her eyes, and they trickled down her cheeks. "No," she said, defiant against the loss of her friend, and then the tears flowed.

She had just started to consider Agrell to be family, and now that was all gone.

"She's dead?" Dozi asked in a small voice.

The two women sat crying together in the low light of the basement for a few minutes before Dozi spoke up again.

"Agrell was only in town a little over a week. She barely got to experience life outside of the cult."

"I didn't even think of that," Ilya replied. "You knew Agrell better than any of the rest of us. You were closest to her," she added. "The mystic and Theolan want us to come to their place, so we can all mourn her together."

"Tell me what happened," Dozi requested.

Ilya recounted everything that she could remember from the rescue mission in the Messiah Tower. She told Dozi about Lahari's powers, and their escape with the prisoners before heading back underground. She also tried to describe a number of the Biological Shifts who possessed particularly memorable appearances. They even discussed the method of disposing the dead for people in the underground.

Ilya then told Dozi about the object that fell from the chimney and caused the underground eruption. Both of them were again brought to tears as Ilya shared what she saw of Agrell's sacrifice, and her flight with Lahari up from the deadly bowels of the underground. Eventually, her tale concluded with their arrival at the apothecary.

When Ilya finished speaking, Dozi tilted her head to one side and looked over to the space that led to her storage area, where the cold air was still blowing into her home.

"I think I should be dead," she commented. "It sounds to me like the crack in the bedrock that Agrell used to get down to the room with the fire well, should have let the poisonous gases from the volcano right up into my home while I was asleep."

"But Agrell said the crack also led out to the water," Ilya replied. "Maybe the fumes were syphoned that way, instead of seeping in here."

"Lucky," Dozi mumbled.

Both of them fell silent again, and their eyes sparkled as tears poured down their cheeks.

Dozi cleared her throat hard. "Come on," she said. "Let's go be sad with friends," and they headed up into the glow of the morning.

Theolan was just coming out of a door in the back room, as the two women arrived at the shop. He was carrying a dusty bottle of champagne. The mystic's eyes were red from already shedding tears, but as soon as he saw Ilya and Dozi, he burst anew with fresh sobs. He rushed over and embraced one and then the other.

"Hello, ladies," Theolan said in a somber tone. He was wearing a smile that did not make it up to his eyes; the expression looked fake, but Dozi and Ilya knew exactly how he felt.

None of them could stop their sorrow. None of them wanted to stop it, and they released their misery together.

Lahari placed five champagne flutes on the countertop, and Theolan began to fill them. The bubbly liquid foamed to the top of the glasses but only trickled over the lip of one.

They cried together, laughed together, talked about the prior week and a half as if it were an entire lifetime. For Agrell, being away from the cult *was* like an entire new life. The five celebrated her through the afternoon and past sundown, and as supper approached, Theolan insisted that they all remain together for the meal.

"Despite where she came from and what she went through," Ilya said, "those things didn't define her. In fact, Agrell was the opposite of what several of us first thought of her, and I for one regret having judged her."

"I think we'll have none of that," Dozi insisted. "Agrell would not want you to hold those thoughts in your heart, especially not when thinking about her. Agrell was *not* where she came from; she was not the Lovegood cult."

"I wish we could go burn it to the ground," Lahari said through her teeth.

Her father turned to her and replied gently. "That would likely only make the followers more zealous."

"I also think," Dozi added, "that Agrell would not want us filling our hearts with hatred, not while we are remembering her."

She continued. "Up in Bluewood, where I'm from in the mountains, we would make dashai for the people we love. Do you know what they are, dashai? It's made from some sort of paste that solidifies, but it's lightweight."

"Oh, yes!" Theolan replied. "I've never heard that term before, but I bet you're talking about glivrock."

"Of course!" his husband added. He turned to Dozi. "I have the ingredients to make a batch. Why don't you tell us about the dashee?" the mystic attempted.

"Dashai," Dozi clarified.

"*Dashai*, thank you, my dear," he dutifully repeated. "Perhaps you can tell us how your village made theirs."

Dozi nodded. "We use a large round metal plate with a lip around the edge and fill it with a thin layer of wet dashai. To harden it, we place it over hot coals, but before it solidifies, we each press our palm print into it. The celebrated person's name is written at the center, and the hands surround it forever. Unless you drop it," she added. "Our neighbor dropped one that was made for their kid. The thing broke apart and they weren't able to repair it."

"We'll take good care of it," Theolan assured her.

"All of our hands should be in it," Dozi said with an assertive tone. She looked around the room from one person to the next. "I think Agrell only experienced twelve days of freedom," and her voice cracked, "before she sacrificed herself." Dozi cleared her throat hard. "But in that short time," she continued before anyone else could interrupt, "she became fast friends with all of us, and she didn't care who we were or what we had done; Agrell made us all her family."

Dozi looked at Ilya. "When we found you at my mushroom cave, you were a damsel in distress, and Agrell was your rescuer. She was someone who everyone else saw as a cannibal, a Messiah, but Agrell was determined to save the life," and she took Ilya's hand, "of a Shift." Dozi chuckled. "I think if I told that to most people, they wouldn't believe me. Agrell was quite fond of you Ilya."

As Dozi spoke, the mystic collected the ingredients to mix, and Theolan grabbed a rectangular metal baking tray.

"I know, it's not round," he said apologetically. He placed it onto the counter next to a large bowl that his husband was filling with several liquid and powder items. "I do think all our hands will fit, and we can pop it into the oven to harden."

Dozi smiled. "I think that'll work perfectly," she replied. She turned and did her best to look at Lahari, her strange face, her yellow eyes. "Agrell treated you in a way that few of us normal people have the capacity." She then caught herself and Dozi dropped her gaze.

"I'm sorry," she said quickly, and she looked back up at Lahari. "I didn't mean that the way it came out, I'm sorry," she repeated.

Lahari replied, "It's okay. I haven't been *normal* for years."

"But thank you, Dozi" Theolan added. "It's important to correct ourselves, to help us grow and become more understanding."

She nodded, took a breath, and continued speaking to Lahari. "Agrell wanted to help you, and to help an entire group of people who would have hated her if they knew who she was."

"Some of them did," Lahari said.

"*You*," Dozi added with strong emphasis on the word, and she stared into Lahari's yellow eyes, "are part of Agrell's family. You belong with us, Lahari. Your handprint needs to be next to ours."

Theolan helped his husband pour the contents of the bowl into the baking tray.

"Let's heat this up for a minute, then press our hands in it and write her name," the mystic recommended.

Dozi turned to him. "I know that Agrell looked up to you. You were like a father figure that she'd never had, and I think she felt a special affinity for you when she learned about Lahari and how accepting you were of her." Dozi looked back at Lahari with a smile. The young woman was still mildly terrifying, but Dozi wanted to accept her in the same way Agrell did.

She brought her gaze to Theolan. "Agrell may have felt like your husband was fatherly to her, but I think she saw you as a big brother. She was so upset after you got beat up, and she mentioned how much it bothered her to us." Dozi indicated Ilya. "Agrell liked you both a lot," she added to the men. "Your hands also need to be in the dashai."

The mystic removed the tray from the heat, and each of them pressed their palms into the lukewarm surface. Sorrow caused fresh tears to spring from their eyes, as the perfect impression of five palm prints formed a line in the dashai.

Dozi wiped her eyes, as the mystic handed her one of the numerous twigs that he sold in his shop for incantations and potions. She used it to spell out Agrell's name above the tips of the fingers, and they returned the tray to the oven.

Theolan dabbed the corners of his eyes and blew his nose.

Lahari and her father shared a handkerchief.

Ilya wiped her tears on her sleeve.

"The dashai only takes a few minutes to become rock hard," Dozi said with a sniffle.

Then she choked, "I didn't even get to say goodbye to her," and Dozi was overcome by sobs. She cried into her hands, and the others gathered around her.

Theolan and the mystic hugged Dozi on either side, and Ilya and Lahari joined the mournful embrace. The five spent a quiet tearful moment together before they separated.

Dozi cleared her throat hard, trying to force her sadness down. "The dashai is probably done," she said.

The mystic removed it from the heat.

"Let it cool and then it should come right out," Dozi instructed. "We should attach a hook to the back and hang it in the front of your shop, if you've got a spot for it."

"I'm sure we can find a nice home for the dashai," the mystic replied.

"It looks good," Dozi added. "Agrell," she said with a smile, but then she gritted her teeth and added under her breath, "fuck," as a fresh wave of tears burned her eyes. "I miss her."✪

Epilogue 1 - Plotting

Later that night, when the two men were upstairs and the three young women were still seated by candlelight, Ilya commented, "What if we just did it ourselves."

The other two looked at her with expectant expressions.

"What do you mean?" Dozi asked.

"Burn it to the ground," Ilya replied.

Lahari nodded. "I'm in."

Dozi frowned at them. "The Lovegoods?" she said in disbelief. "You know they're all Messiahs, right? How on earth do you think it would be possible to do that without getting caught and killed yourselves?"

Ilya looked at Lahari.

Dozi shook her head. "And what about the innocent people who might die in the fire?" she continued. "People like Agrell before she escaped, or children that were born into the cult. What if there are others who have tried to get away but were caught and are still there?"

"I wish Agrell were alive," Ilya said, and she choked down the lump that started to rise in her throat. She looked at Lahari. "If we are going to do this, we need someone with intimate knowledge about the cult."

"I know someone," Lahari replied.

*

It was determined by the inhabitants of the underground that their home was destroyed. The magma did not rise as high as the newly appointed Principal Messiah hoped. However, it flowed into many of the deep chambers, and much of the impressive original excavations by the old Oselian military were filled by the magma. The liquid slowly cooled and solidified into igneous rock, and it again became part of the peninsula's bedrock upon which Teshon City sat, but most of the underground no longer existed ★

Epilogue 2 - Breakfast

As the morning sun began to slide up the cloud-shrouded sky, *many* voices were shouting in anger.

"Oi! Shut it!"

"Will you please shut up?!"

"Stop yelling!"

"Do you know what time it is?!"

Dozi was standing outside the mystic's apothecary, calling up to their closed window. It was early, but she was trying to rouse the sleeping men. She did her best to ignore the other groggy inhabitants of the neighborhood who were upset with her.

"What is that ruckus?!"

"Shut up!"

"Who's making all that noise?!"

"You woke me up!"

This was too serious; Dozi just needed to wake the men, and then everything would be fine. It seemed that she had disturbed everyone in the vicinity, except for the two she was trying to awaken.

"Shut up!!"

"Great, now my baby is screaming!"

"Keep it down!"

"What the fuck is wrong with you?!"

The window above Dozi opened and Theolan's head popped out.

"What is going on out here?" he mumbled.

"Let me in!" Dozi shrieked. "Let me inside!"

A moment later, she was in the shop and the mystic was making three cups of tea for breakfast.

"We don't have time for that!" Dozi barked at him. "They left! I didn't think they were serious last night, but they're gone! *And* they've got a major head start on us," Dozi seemed frantic; she was normally so easygoing.

"Slow down, what are you talking about?" Theolan asked.

Dozi grunted at the men in frustration. "They're gone!" she repeated. "Ilya and Lahari got this crazy notion last night, and they recruited Auntie Peg to get revenge for Agrell or something, and they left at dawn. They are going to the cult!"

The mystic looked puzzled and said, "That doesn't make any sense. They can't have gone."

"What are you talking about?" Dozi snapped. "Why the fuck have I been out there waking up the whole neighborhood? Of course, they're gone; I didn't make it up!"

"Okay, okay," Theolan said, trying to appease her, "tell us what happened."

"I don't know if they are planning on attacking the cult or what, but there was mention of setting it on fire!"

"It's going to take them days to get there," Theolan commented. He looked apprehensive. "My grandparents were from Eckelton, and I visited there, but it was years ago." He looked into Dozi's eyes. "The three of them are really going to walk all the way to the Lovegood cult, in order to kill people, all in remembrance of Agrell?"

"That's what *I* said! Like our dashai meant nothing," Dozi grumbled.

"No, I'm sure it's not like that," the mystic cajoled. "The dashai we made for her last night was a very sweet moment for the five of us."

"And now, they plan murder in the name of Agrell," Dozi concluded in a dry voice❂

Epilogue 3 - Journey

Ilya, Lahari, and Auntie Peg walked out through the Teshon City gates. The morning sun was climbing the early-winter sky behind a veil of grey clouds. It was cold, and the three travelers were all bundled heavily, but none more so than Lahari.

Every inch of her unique, scaly blue-grey skin was covered. She wore a thick jacket and trousers with boots and gloves. A knit cap and scarf hid her head, and dark snow goggles prevented anyone from seeing her yellow eyes. However, Lahari was not used to wearing clothing, and she was uncomfortable.

The trio followed road signs and walked along with a number of other people on the Southtrack towards the village of Brokenpointe. They stayed their first night at an inn, overlooking the sea.

Once they were in their private room, Lahari declared, "I've got to get out of all this!"

She groaned, and the other two women could not help but stare at her, as she peeled the layers of clothes off her unique body. As she stripped naked, her black quills lifted from her skin and flexed, and she moved in place. Lahari stretched and extended her arms, bent her knees and squatted down, and she twisted her spine like a snake. It was as if the movement was cleansing her from the clothing.

All the while, her quills were in motion, and they were mesmerizing to Auntie Peg and Ilya. The black spines shifted in fluid unison and appeared to the two other women as rippling patterns that moved over Lahari's unique body. Then she stood upright again, and the beautiful spines fell still.

Her eyes moved to Auntie Peg and Ilya. "Sorry," she said, before either of them could apologize for staring. "I suddenly realize that we should have gotten food before I made myself comfortable."

"Oh, don't you worry about that," Auntie Peg replied in an encouraging tone. "I will tell the barkeep that you are exhausted from our trip, and I will bring food up for you to eat, and you don't have to be seen."

Auntie Peg smiled. "By the by," she added, as she stepped up to the door and turned the handle; she looked back toward Lahari, "we didn't mean to gawk at you, but you are so beautiful, child," and she and Ilya left her alone.

Lahari was startled by the kind words and stood staring at the closed door. It was one thing for her fathers to compliment her, but even *she* thought of herself as monstrous.

Beautiful, she thought. *Beautiful?*

Noise from down on the beach outside drew her attention to the window. Lahari doused the lights and peered out at the ocean. The water looked black beneath the moonless sky, and she gazed into its rolling darkness. Commotion caught her eye and she looked down closer to the building.

A drum kit was set up on a wooden riser. There was a person seated behind it, adjusting each percussive instrument to the right position. Two other people joined the drummer, and a moment later, music began to swirl up from the beach.

Lahari raised the window a crack to hear it better, and the room began to cool. A radiator hissed to life in the corner, spreading its warmth against the cold.

There was a knock on the door and Auntie Peg's voice called out, "It's just me, dear." She entered and shut it behind her. "Supper is a hearty stew!"

"I'm watching the band," Lahari declared in a bright voice. Her yellow eyes were wide with wonder. "I want to eat by the window."

"I think that's a marvelous idea," Auntie Peg agreed. "Lights off was a good idea, too."

"I know you're also hungry," Lahari said as she took the steaming bowl and placed it on a small table. "I'm good, and you should head back down to eat." She then turned to Auntie Peg. "Oh," Lahari said as if she forgot something, "thank you!"

"Not a problem, my dear," Auntie Peg replied with a chuckle. She handed Lahari a large chunk of crusty bread before returning down to join Ilya.

However, Auntie Peg was not pleased to see a trio of fishermen who were seated at the table around Ilya. They were all leering at her with lecherous desire.

Auntie Peg stepped right up, wedged herself between Ilya and the nearest man, and managed to shove him back from her.

"My, my, my," she commented in a very ladylike tone, but loud, "this table's gotten a bit crowded."

"We like where we're…"

"I was not speaking to you." Auntie Peg interrupted. She stared dead into his eyes. Her face was expressionless.

Another tried to interject. "Hey now, we were just…"

"What you were just doing was intimidating a girl," Auntie Peg snapped.

Other guests were starting to pay attention, and the band stopped playing.

"Only weak little wormy boys try to win women through fear. We have no interest in your advances, nor whatever you were going to try and pressure her into doing."

"We wanted to…"

"We want *none* of what you're offering," Auntie Peg said over him. "Be on your way," and she added, "now."

The three men looked around at the other tables, where customers were all silent and staring at them. Without the cover of music mixed with countless conversations, the men rose, grumbling under their breath. They did not look happy, but they headed down to the beach, and the chatter around the patio returned.

"How did you do that?" Ilya asked. "You insulted them right to their faces." She added with a little awe in her voice. "I could never."

"Well," Auntie Peg replied with a guilty expression, "not only am I a *man* under all this glamour, and I've been in more than a few altercations over the years, but also this…" and she nodded down towards her large traveling purse on her lap.

Through the opening, Ilya could see that in one hand Auntie Peg gripped the hilt of a dagger, and in the other, she held a purple glass sphere.

"I was prepared," she informed Ilya. "This is sleep powder. It would have taken out the two who were seated on the other side of you, and the man next to me would not have been the first person I've stabbed, although I'm glad I didn't need to stab anyone on this lovely evening."

Auntie Peg and Ilya sat uninterrupted for the remainder of their time on the patio. Around them, folks ate and drank and talked and laughed, with the night enveloping the land in darkness.

The local Brokenpointe musicians entertained the patrons, and roaring fires on either side of the riser where the band performed added a bizarre glow that illuminated the players. A third fire burned merrily in a fireplace built into the patio, and it helped to warm the tavern's guests on that chilly winter night.

Auntie Peg rose from the table and left Ilya where she was seated. When she returned, she was carrying three tankards of ale. "I'm going to bring one up to our other friend, be right back."

She climbed the stairs, knocked on the door, and called out, "It's me again!" as she turned the key in the lock. The door opened, and it was dark in the room, but Lahari's yellow eyes glowed at Auntie Peg.

"Thought you'd enjoy a mug of beer as you listen to the music."

"I love it!" Lahari declared.

Auntie Peg furrowed her brow. "But you haven't even tried it yet," she replied, extending the beverage to Lahari.

"No, the music!" Lahari said, and she laughed with delight. She took a sip. "Ooh, that's good, too," she added. Auntie Peg picked up the empty dish, and Lahari said, "Please, stay down there as long as you'd like. There's no rush. I'm really enjoying the music."

Auntie Peg chuckled and replied, "We probably won't stay late. It's been a big day."

Downstairs, Ilya was enjoying her ale when Auntie Peg joined her again. They sat together with their drinks, and when they were done, the two women decided to call it a night. The band was still playing as they rose, but they settled their tab and headed back upstairs.

"Us again," Auntie Peg called as she opened the door to the dark room.

Lahari was staring down at the musicians.

"Do you mind if we turn the lights on for a bit?" Auntie Peg asked her. "Maybe just scoot back from view, or even sit beneath the window while the lights are on?" she recommended.

Lahari obliged and shifted herself to the floor.

"Well," Auntie Peg said to her traveling companions, "I guess it's *my* turn to get dramatic." She laughed and lifted her wig off of her head.

Both Lahari and Ilya were surprised to see the smushed pale blonde hair beneath. It was short and unkempt. Auntie Peg ran her long nails through it a few times and sighed. Then she peeled off her lash extensions and began to wash her face.

"Ugh!" she exclaimed. "It's getting so basic in this mirror." She peered at the reflective glass. Water dripped from her chin and makeup streaked her cheeks. "The boy beneath begins to emerge," Auntie Peg added with a smirk, "but he's not nearly as much fun."

"What's your real name?" Ilya asked.

Auntie Peg turned and extended her arm toward Ilya with a wide smile. Her makeup was gone, and beneath it she was very plain-looking. Auntie Peg was slender and effeminate, but there really *was* a 40 year old man underneath. Her and Ilya's hands connected.

"I'm so pleased to meet you," Auntie Peg said jokingly. She added, "The name I was given at birth is Bizzle Lovegood, but *Auntie Peg* or *Peggy* is who I really am."

"Wow," Ilya whispered in disbelief, and Auntie Peg smirked. "Sorry," Ilya blurted out, "I didn't mean to say that aloud." Then she turned to Lahari. "Have you ever seen him like this?"

"I think *she* is what Peggy prefers," Lahari responded, "and no, I haven't."

Neither Ilya nor Auntie Peg could decipher Lahari's expression, but she was also staring.

"Ta-da!" Auntie Peg said, putting her hands up by her cheeks and framing her face. "A boy," she stated with another bright smile, "and she's exhausted," she added. "Let's turn in."

She leaned towards Ilya. "When I'm all done up, I certainly expect to be addressed by everyone as *she*, but like this," and Auntie Peg struck a pose, "you can call me he or she."

A moment later, the lights were out again. Auntie Peg let Ilya and Lahari take the two beds, and she wrapped herself in a blanket on the couch. Lahari did not want to shut out the lovely sounds of the music, and Auntie Peg and Ilya were happy to leave the window cracked, even though it let in the chilly air. The heater periodically hissed to life and pushed back the cold.

"Good night and sweet dreams, ladies," Auntie Peg said, and soon she and Ilya were fast asleep.

Lahari lay awake, listening to the music, but other noises began to interrupt her enjoyment.

Multiple voices shouting hateful remarks began a discordant cacophony over the song. The slurred speech and bravado that came with inebriation was so disruptive that the musicians stopped playing.

Lahari heard the words *bitch* and *slut*, but she could not make out where the anger was directed. She sat up in the darkness and looked at the window, but from the bed, she could only see out to sea. She slinked over to look down at the beach, and she saw three men stomping around the patio.

"They're gone," someone said below.

"Where'd they go?" a drunken voice managed to enunciate.

Then the barkeep spoke up. "Look, fellas, why don't I give you each a beer on the house, and you take it and head on your way? Huh, what do you say to that? There no need for trouble."

"What if we're looking for trouble?" one of them sneered, and he knocked over a table with a few empty plates. They crashed to the floor and shattered.

Another of the drunkards grabbed the bartender by his collar. "Are they staying here? You know who I'm talking about, the woman with the smart mouth from earlier and her young friend. We want a word with them."

Lahari looked over at Auntie Peg's sleeping frame.

"I can't tell you if they're staying here!" the barkeep replied.

The man released his shirt and said, "That confirms it, boys. Them bitches are upstairs. Let's find 'em and drag 'em down to the beach."

They started roaring drunken obscenities over any words of protest from other guests, and the men entered the building through the patio doors. They made quite a ruckus, knocking over and smashing a few more plates and glasses from a side table.

Lahari closed the window, crept to the door, and opened it a crack. The hall was empty, but she could hear the men stomping up the stairs. She slipped out and gently pushed the door so that it was not quite closed and did not latch. Then she moved toward the top of the stairs and the oncoming group of men.

"What in the fucking..." the one at the front began to say, as he came face to face with Lahari. He froze and the other men bumped into him.

Lahari reached her arms forward, and he leaned back.

"What the hell are you doing?" one of them snapped.

"I almossht lossht my balancsh," the other mumbled.

The man in front grunted an indistinguishable syllable of disgust, as Lahari's blue scaly hands came to either side of his face. Then he went rigid and wheezed the air out of his lungs. Before his companions' eyes, he began to vaporize. He could not even scream, as the molecules of his body began to break down to their elemental parts. Atomic bonds failed, and in a split second, his life fled the shell of his body. His form became like a cold cinder that was burned down to ash, and what remained of him crumbled to a pile of dust on the stairs.

The other two men screamed in terror at the instantaneous death and disintegration, but they were silenced.

Lahari reached out and grabbed both of them.

One man slipped from her grip and fell backward. Her powers affected humans even more horribly than they did to either Messiahs or Demifae. He was dead before he fell back. As his form tumbled down the stairs, first an arm and then a leg broke off, and finally his head separated from his body. He landed at the bottom of the flight in a pile of dried-out chunks.

Lahari pulled the final man against her body, stabbing into his flesh with her needle-sharp black quills, and she wrapped her arms around him. Then she unleashed her full power and the man vanished.

Lahari relaxed again, and a faint wisp of steam curled up towards the ceiling and dissipated.

The hall above the stairs was still empty, and Lahari sneaked back into the room ★

Epilogue 4 - The End

Auntie Peg was all done up in her traveling finest again. She, Ilya, and Lahari were halfway between Brokenpointe and Eckelton when Lahari told them about her encounter the night before with the three men. There were no other travelers on the road to the tiny village, and the scarf she wore to hide her face was pulled down.

"I killed them," Lahari concluded.

"What do you mean? Where were the bodies this morning?" Auntie Peg asked her.

"Their bodies disappeared."

"What do you think they were going to do with us?" Ilya asked.

"And what would they have done with me?" Lahari added, waving a gloved hand by the side of her face and indicating her otherworldly appearance. "They were bad people, right?" she asked. Both Ilya and Auntie Peg made uncertain faces at her. "Fuck a redemption story," Lahari added.

"And now they can't harass anyone else," Ilya added to Auntie Peg. She turned to Lahari. "You should've seen how she sent them on their way last night."

"Yeah," Lahari replied, "but they came back worse. They seemed pretty agro when they got there. Who knows what shit they've done to others before, or what they intended with you two. Fuck redemption," she repeated, and she pulled her scarf up over her face.

Auntie Peg sighed.

"What is it?" Ilya asked her.

"I'm just thinking," she replied. "It's nothing."

Ilya looked up at the trees. "How much farther through these woods do you think this path goes?"

"The sun is still high," Auntie Peg replied. "We aren't supposed to make it to Eckelton until after sunset, so I bet we've got a ways to go still."

They walked for a while in silence, and before long, the pale sun began to set.

"Can't wait to get there," Auntie Peg commented. "They better have rooms for us. Take my hands, girls. Stay close." She hooked her hands into both their elbows.

The forest was quiet under the darkening sky.

"I'm sorry," Auntie Peg said to them, "for Agrell. I'm sorry she's gone." She sucked air through her teeth. "Gotta keep it together," she said to herself, and she choked down the lump in her throat. "Don't ruin your makeup," Auntie Peg commanded herself.

She continued. "I know that you both spent a lot of time with her during her few days of freedom. Thank you for accepting her, even knowing where she came from," and she added, "where *I* came from."

Then through the blackness ahead of them, a twinkling became visible through the trees.

"Oh, good," Ilya said. "We finally made it. I'm famished."

The path rounded some trees, and the glimpses of light became the old tired town of Eckelton. Torches and lamps burned at the front of the two taverns.

The three weary travelers approached one, and Auntie Peg opened the door.

A man with a handlebar mustache greeted them. "Hello there, ladies, and welcome to The Crossed Swords. Will you three be needing rooms, or are you just here for supper?"

"We'd love a room, one for me and my girls," Auntie Peg replied. "We are exhausted and hungry."

The mustachioed man smiled. "I can certainly accommodate you. Why don't you head up to the room, and I'll get some food ready for you?"

"That sounds marvelous."

Their host then shouted, "*Zilly!*"

A burly teenage boy who was built like a stone wall walked out from the back room.

"Take these ladies' bags up to suite four." He turned back to his three guests. "I apologize for the climb, but the rooms that can accommodate more than one person are on the third floor. Please, follow Zilly."

"Not a problem," Auntie Peg assured him. She handed her bag to the muscular boy with a flirty smile.

Once they were in their room, Auntie Peg opened the door a crack and watched him head back downstairs. "Mama likey," she purred under her breath. "He's gone…" She shut the door.

Lahari started pulling off her excessive clothes and stripped naked to her scaly blue-grey skin. She again flexed all her quills in rippling patterns, and the other two women watched her. When Lahari was satisfied, she looked back at them.

"Sorry!" Auntie Peg blurted out. "We don't mean to stare at you, but child, you are stunning. You really are quite beautiful."

Lahari was not accustomed to praise, and she looked down at her hands, as if an explanation for Auntie Peg's kindness was in her palms.

Ilya and Auntie Peg removed their outer layers and headed back to the door.

"I'll bring you up some food in a few minutes," Auntie Peg said, and they were gone.

Agrell entered Lahari's thoughts. She collapsed to her knees, clutched her heart, and tears flooded from her yellow eyes. The sobs shook her body. She was unaccustomed to crying but overcome with sorrow.

She was still crouched on the floor when Ilya knocked on the door.

"It's me this time," she called out, and she opened it. "Oh, Lahari!" she cried. Ilya quickly placed the plate of food onto the table and dropped down beside the trembling woman. She placed her palm against a bare patch of Lahari's shoulder.

"*Don't touch me!*" Lahari wailed, and she pulled away.

Ilya screamed out in pain, as her knuckles were sliced open by a few of Lahari's black quills.

Lahari turned, and Ilya cowered away from her. She clutched her bloody hand and looked terrified.

"I'm sorry!" Lahari cried, and she wrapped her arms around Ilya. Her spines relaxed and softened. "I'm sorry, I'm sorry," she repeated over and over. She jumped up and grabbed a towel to tie around Ilya's bloody knuckles. "I'm so sorry," Lahari said again. Tears were pouring from her yellow eyes. "It's just…" she paused, and she choked a sob as she said, *Agrell!"*

The two young women wrapped their arms around each other, and they cried for long minutes together. Lahari's spines even seemed to softly caress Ilya as they hugged.

Eventually, they rose from the floor, and Ilya left Lahari alone. She joined Auntie Peg downstairs.

When the two returned to the room, Auntie Peg knocked and said at the crack of the door, "It's us!" and they entered.

Auntie Peg was wearing a sad expression, and she asked Lahari, "May I hug you?" and the two embraced. "I'm so sorry about Agrell."

Lahari squeezed Auntie Peg tight and growled into her shoulder, "Stop making me cry!"

"It's okay to let it out," Auntie Peg comforted in a gentle voice. "I know that I barely got to know Agrell, but she was lucky to have had you in her life while she was a free woman. Your heart is big, Lahari," Auntie Peg added.

Ilya stood off to one side, and she sniffed hard to fight back her tears.

Auntie Peg looked over at her and said, "Come here, child." She extended one arm and welcomed Ilya into her embrace, and the three women cried for their friend.

"Maybe," Auntie Peg ventured, "our trip is more about this than vengeance."✪

Epilogue 5 - The Beginning

"We know what you're planning," Dozi declared, "and we're here to stop you!" She came stomping down the path that led into Eckelton with the mystic and Theolan behind her.

The sun was rising. For most of the season, grey clouds hung above Teshon City and the surrounding area, but the sky was clear that morning. The winter haze would soon return.

Auntie Peg and Ilya were seated at a table in the sun. Plates were in front of them, and the two looked up from their food toward the three frazzled travelers.

Dozi was frowning.

Auntie Peg raised one hand and gave them a dainty wave. "Would you like some breakfast?" she asked.

The mystic looked exhausted, but he perked up at the prospect of food.

Dozi replied, "You're not going to dissuade us. We are here to prevent you from doing what I know you have planned."

"Lahari is up in our room," Auntie Peg commented with a lovely smile. "You boys should go say good morning to her before joining us."

"I'm serious," Dozi said emphatically. "Don't do this, please. Don't do what you think you need to do."

"We already know," replied Ilya.

"What do you mean?" Dozi asked her.

Ilya gave her an apologetic smile. "I mean, we know you're right. We came to the same conclusion."

"I think we just needed to grieve Agrell," Auntie Peg added, "in our own way. Sorry we worried you, dear. And I agree with Ilya, you're right." Auntie Peg reached out and took Dozi's hand. "Thank you," she said, "for believing in what was right, and for coming after us. Agrell was lucky to have known you."

Tears sprang to Dozi's eyes, and Auntie Peg leapt to her feet and wrapped her in a tight embrace. Even though Dozi did not know the woman, she broke down and exploded, sobbing against her shoulder.

As Dozi cried, Auntie Peg whispered, "Ilya, why don't you take the boys up to see Lahari?" and they entered the tavern.

Dozi's body trembled. Her knees were weak, but Auntie Peg hugged her.

"It's okay, girl," she comforted, as tears welled at the corner of her own eyes. "Great, now you're gonna make me cry, too."

The two women held each other as the sun slowly crept up the pale winter sky.

"Wait a second," Auntie Peg said. "Did you three walk all night?" she asked.

Dozi could not speak through her shuddering breaths, but she nodded against Auntie Peg's chest.

"Oh, child, you must care deeply, to have convinced the boys to walk all night, in order to stop the three of us on our path of revenge. Thank you," Auntie Peg said to Dozi again, "for taking good care of Agrell."

Theolan reappeared with Ilya, and they both sat, as Dozi pulled herself from Auntie Peg's embrace. She sniffed hard and wiped her eyes, then she also sat at the table.

Auntie Peg and Ilya continued their breakfast, and Dozi and Theolan ordered their own meals. He also ordered a plate of food for the mystic.

Lahari and her father came outside and joined the rest of their group. She was covered from head to toe.

Auntie Peg and Ilya finished eating, and the two of them rose. Lahari and Ilya meandered down the dusty street, as Auntie Peg headed back in to the inn's front desk.

"Any chance we can rent the room for several more hours? A few friends of ours traveled through the night and just arrived this morning. I'd love to let them rest a while before we head out on the road again."

She negotiated the price for a half-day extra and then headed back outside. She informed Dozi and the men that after their sleepless night, they could use the room and nap through the morning. After the others ate, Auntie Peg escorted them to the room.

"This isn't a ploy to get rid of us and go have your revenge, is it?" Dozi questioned.

"No," Auntie Peg said with a chuckle, "those feelings are gone. Again, I'm sorry we worried you. We'll be waiting outside when you three are feeling rested."

She joined Lahari and Ilya out under the weak winter sun, and the three of them strolled arm in arm through the tiny town.

A few of the townsfolk were out and about, enjoying the mild day, and several people stopped to chat with the three ladies. They discussed the weather, what crops grew in the area, or how many generations of families had lived there in town. It was pleasant and meaningless banter that helped to pass the time.

The sun was reaching its low zenith in the winter sky when the others emerged from the inn.

They ate a second meal in front of the tavern, enjoying the weak warmth and the clear day. When they finished, Auntie Peg headed inside and settled up with the host. She returned with a small box of artisanal chocolate truffles that were handmade by the resident chef.

"Well, isn't that delightful?" the mystic said.

Each of them took one, and an extra remained in the box.

They all slowly devoured their treats, savoring the sweet and subtle bitterness of the chocolate.

Auntie Peg licked her fingertips, as she held up the box with the final truffle.

"That one should have been for Agrell," Dozi said, and she smothered a sob that threatened its way up her throat.

Several of them were brought to tears, and the group again comforted each other. All of them passed on having a second chocolate.

Dabbing his eyes with his handkerchief, the mystic double-checked with everyone else that they did not want the last truffle, and he ate it.

Then the six of them turned their backs to Eckelton and began the journey home ★

Also by Adam Andrews Johnson

The Mantis Equilibrium - Book Two
Someone is slaughtering Messiahs, and the
Messiahs are investigating. Who will survive this
new confrontation and what will be left of them?
Featuring:
GODS, DRAGONS, & DRAG QUEENS!

The Mantis Corruption - Book Three
In the east are MONSTERS. To the north is the
WITCH. In the south lies the CAPITAL. To the west
is the WASTE. The land is called XIN.
How is this distant land connected to the people
and events in Books One & Two? And what will
happen with the monsters?

The Mantis Continuum - Book Four
A story of eldritch horror and psychic
confrontations. Two weird children go through a
significant upheaval in their happy lives. A unique
trio of gay 17 year old lads embark on a buccaneer
adventure. A man living alone in isolation is found
and helped, but with very unexpected
consequences.

Coming in 2024 from Danu Books
A sexy new tale begins!

The Starting End - Book One
An epic fantasy adventure in a queer normative
universe. The Starting End is a spicy exploration of
unique kinks and relationships, and love is
experienced in a plethora of beautiful ways.
Gender identity and sexuality are celebrated
through the diverse cast of characters who come
from across the LGBTQIA+ rainbow.

Adam Andrews Johnson

177